ABOUT BREE VERITY

Bree Verity grew up on a diet of tea and crumpets, dancing, Regency novels, old movies and musicals. It's no wonder she has ended up writing love stories.

She lives in Perth Western Australia with her teenage son, her long-suffering, patient and wonderful partner, and her two doggy writing buddies, Millie and Boofie. She keeps it very quiet from them that she is equally a cat person.

She loves watching sci-fi and renovation shows (usually not together, however sometimes the Doctor redecorates...), reading historical and time travel books, hanging out with her local community theatre, and sleeping in.

When someone discovers the way to directly infuse tea into the veins, she will volunteer immediately as a guinea pig.

Bree loves to hear from her readers, and can be contacted on Facebook or Twitter, or at her website www.breeverity.com where you can also sign up for her monthly newsletter.

MORE TITLES FROM BREE VERITY

The Hidden Duchess
The Ruined Lady - pre-order now for release on 17 October 2017

The Perth Girls series
For Business and Pleasure
Troubled by the Texan - pre-order now for release on 17 Sept 2017
Under the Spotlight - coming soon

A Bouquet of Love - anthology

DEDICATION

To my sisters, Anjanette and Farrah,
And to my Mum, Denise,
For all of us going on the Georgette Heyer journey together
And for all of us falling in love with the Scarlet Pimpernel
And for all the old swashbuckling movies we used to watch
That made me want to write this kind of novel.
I love you.

PROLOGUE

Jean de Lacey's breath was harsh in his chest as he crashed through the underbrush. Far too close behind him, another man struggled through as well—the new exciseman brought in to try to curb the smuggling trade along the Kent coast.

De Lacey didn't want to kill him. He had never killed anyone and didn't want to start now, but the exciseman could possibly recognize him and point him out to the local magistrate. De Lacey could never let that happen.

He stopped for a moment, letting the other man get closer, then he pulled his pistol and fired a shot in the officer's direction.

"What the devil?" The exciseman stopped, unsure from where exactly the shot had come.

The air was still, even the birds and insects silenced by the gunfire. De Lacey held his breath and ignored the bead of perspiration that trickled down his face. He wanted to creep away, to forget all about smuggling, to go and live his life in London until he could return to France. But that was impossible now.

Another shot rang out. A yelp of pain. Branches snapping and crunching underfoot as someone got closer and closer. De Lacey swallowed. This was it then. He set his feet, pistol held out in front of him, refusing to notice that his hand was shaking.

Then, the bushes parted, and a figure ran out, halting at the sight of de Lacey's gun.

"Don't shoot, Jean. It's me."

De Lacey sighed in relief at Jack Finchley, one of his co-conspirators. "Where is the excise?" he asked.

"Winged him," replied Jack confidently. "He's turned back, I'm sure."

De Lacey sagged. Once again, he had managed to outrun the authorities. He panted, his hands resting on his knees.

"Never again," he said to Jack, straightening up. "I am never doing this again."

Jack chuckled. "You always say that, but you're always here."

"Never again."

Jack threw a companionable arm over de Lacey's shoulder. "Well, while you decide, Jean, we should head toward The Ancient Crow. There'll be a pretty party there tonight."

De Lacey scowled at his young companion and trudged back through the underbrush. He should have quit this smuggling racket years ago. It was time to get out.

The only problem was persuading his fellow smugglers to allow him to do so.

CHAPTER ONE

London
March 1793

"Brandy, Markham, if you please."

With a bow, the superior butler at Brooks's withdrew silently, leaving the two gentlemen to settle into their winged-back leather and mahogany chairs, one with the ease of a wealthy and successful man, and the other a little furtively, glancing at the other club members from under his fine, dark brows. Once he was settled, the gentleman reached into his inner coat pocket and retrieved a letter, which he read with a growing softness in his eyes. The letter was worn along its folds, the paper thin from much handling.

"News from home?" Lord Edenburgh indicated the letter with a nod of his head as he lit his pipe and started to puff, letting the smoke exit his mouth in a long, satisfied sigh as he leaned back in his chair. He picked up a newspaper from the small table beside him and flicked it open.

"No, I haven't heard anything since war was declared." Jean de Lacey folded up the old letter and put it back in his coat pocket. "It's been difficult to get mail across the Channel."

Edenburgh nodded and murmured his agreement as Markham returned bearing two glasses of brandy which he quietly and deftly transferred to the table between the two gentlemen. "Will there be anything else, my lord?" When Edenburgh shook his head, the butler bowed and withdrew.

For a few moments, the two friends enjoyed the silence of each others' company and the convivial surrounds at Brooks's. During this time of the afternoon, there was a low murmur of conversation and little noise from the gaming tables. Most of the players had taken themselves home to sleep for a few hours before they would return to the tables later in the evening.

"Now, de Lacey, your message left me extremely curious. A matter of some delicacy you said? What, exactly, brings us to Brooks's today?" Lord Edenburgh folded the newspaper in his lap and sat back, his eyes resting on the slightly rakish countenance of his friend.

De Lacey sighed, attempting to let the ambiance of Brooks's wash over him and calm his racing heart, but it was to no avail. His task today was unpleasant but necessary. He sat forward in his chair, his eyes darting everywhere except to his friend's face.

"*Mon ami*, we have been friends for many years, *hein*?"

"Indeed," agreed Lord Edenburgh, chuckling. "Ever since you saved me from that encounter with the Spanish senora."

Despite his errand, de Lacey had to smile. "She was very feisty, *certainement*. She would have eaten you alive." He allowed his mind to dwell on the memory of Dona Maria Constanta's womanly curves for a moment, before returning to the task at hand. "I was hoping that I could… utilize the credit of our friendship to secure some funds from you. A loan, of course. Until my property is returned to me." De Lacey colored and looked around. While he had almost whispered his request, he knew at Brooks's the walls had ears. But none of the other gentlemen appeared to show any interest in de Lacey and Lord Edenburgh.

Of all the things de Lacey thought he might be doing during his exile in London, begging his friends for money had never entered his mind.

"My dear fellow," replied Lord Edenburgh, leaning forward and patting de Lacey's knee. "Say no more. I'll direct my bankers to make a draft to your benefit."

"*Merci*, Quincey. You have taken a great weight off my mind."

De Lacey exhaled a breath he didn't even know he had been holding and smiled.

Lord Edenburgh picked up his newspaper and opened it. "I see the Prince has returned to Carlton House," he remarked. "We can expect the season to become even more hectic now."

De Lacey gratefully accepted the change of topic. "I already have so many invitations. I don't know what to do with them all." He spread his hands and raised an eyebrow. With his handsome countenance, foreign accent, and scurrilous reputation, de Lacey was a hit in London society.

It was disconcerting to de Lacey, this celebrity. He had done nothing to earn it, except cross the Channel when his life was endangered. And now that he was safe in England; it seemed a cowardly act, certainly not brave or romantic, and certainly not one that should earn him accolades. But the British, they were difficult to understand at the best of times. They made heroes out of the strangest of people.

Lord Edenburgh's laugh booming around the quiet room brought de Lacey back to the present. "I myself have managed to squeeze as many as eight invitations into a single evening. I had to take the next two days off to recuperate, but there was little of consequence occurring, so I was not concerned."

"Eight?" De Lacey shook his head, even as his voice betrayed his admiration for his friend's feat. "How is it even possible?"

"I will admit to including a family supper in the count. However, I felt justified in doing so since some young ladies of my sister's acquaintance were also present. But, it took much planning and inconvenience, and I don't suppose I should like to do it again."

De Lacey regarded his friend with affection. Lord Edenburgh was not a portly gentleman; however, it was evident from his chosen pursuits that he preferred the comfort of his chair at Brooks's to the more athletic pastimes that some of the other upper-class gentlemen enjoyed. Lord Edenburgh could be seen playing cards or billiards, and attending many of the sittings of parliament. He was not one to race his curricle along the London

Road, or chase actresses on Drury Lane. All in all, Lord Edenburgh was the very essence of a well-to-do earl approaching middle age.

"I don't suppose you would," replied de Lacey. "I myself could manage only three, maybe four." He drained the last of his brandy and considered the bottom of his glass as if seeking some kind of absolution. "And even those I have to press myself to attend."

"My dear fellow, whatever do you mean?"

De Lacey smiled grimly into his glass. "I will admit, Quincey, I find it difficult to be gay when I am only too aware of the hardships facing my fellowmen across the Channel. I feel a little…" He gave an impatient wave of his hand. "*Impotent*, sitting here with my brandy and my never-ending soirees, knowing my friends are being slaughtered and my lands desecrated."

"Ah." Lord Edenburgh nodded his understanding. He had known de Lacey for quite a few years—since they were both youths on the Grand Tour. De Lacey knew the frustration in his tone would be loud in Edenburgh's ear.

"You need to find yourself a distraction, my dear fellow. I have heard that Lady Portersby has taken quite a fancy to you. Care to try your luck in that direction?" He raised his eyebrows in a comical fashion and de Lacey's face lit up with a genuine smile.

"Actually, Quincey, I'm attempting to give all that up."

"Eh? What was that?" Lord Edenburgh's mouth dropped open.

"I know, I know." De Lacey said, slumping his shoulders. "All of the ladies I could be pursuing. But I had much time to think in the past months, and I've decided to, what is the saying, turn over a green leaf?" He held out his hand and turned it over, palm up.

"A new leaf," corrected Lord Edenburgh, shaking his head. "I can hardly believe it, my good fellow. What has happened to you?"

De Lacey's long and glorious reputation as a libertine preceded him. He had always had a great love for women—sometimes several of them at once. But now he just shrugged.

"Old age, perhaps, or wisdom? I see my friends happily settled, and I begin to wonder."

"Wonder? About what?"

"Whether I will ever be blessed with such happiness as I see in them." De Lacey shifted uncomfortably, the conversation dislodging memories he thought long locked away. Memories of a beautiful red-haired woman whose fine, soft skin belied the strength of the woman underneath. The only woman de Lacey had ever thought he might marry. The woman who was now happily ensconced with her farmer husband in rural France was whose letter de Lacey carried on him at all times. He did not envy Celeste's husband. But he did berate himself for allowing her to get away.

"So, you're seeking a wife then?" Lord Edenburgh's question brought de Lacey back to the present with a start.

"*Mon dieu! Absolument pas.* My situation..."

"Your situation, as you call it, is exactly what draws all the ladies to your side, my dear fellow. If you are seeking a wife, I would advise no better time than now to secure one."

De Lacey shook his head. While he knew he was viewed as some kind of romanticized hero for escaping his country, in truth he felt far from heroic. Even without the cost of keeping a chateau, life in London was expensive. His manservant, Tatillion, continually groaned at the state of his clothing, which was well on the way to becoming threadbare.

And apart from that, he had other extracurricular activities that precluded him from seeking a wife.

"No, *mon ami*, I do not look for a wife at this time. I'm afraid the current crop of English Roses has not produced a single bloom which I should like to pluck."

Lord Edenburgh's laugh bounced around the room again. "By God, de Lacey, you have a way with words. Perhaps you'd prefer to pluck them, eh, instead of marrying them?"

"I already told you, I'm leaving that life behind." De Lacey almost snapped the words at his friend, before closing his eyes and gently pinching the bridge of his nose. "Forgive me, Quincey; I'm not quite myself this afternoon."

"You haven't been yourself since you showed up on my

doorstep three years ago," remarked Lord Edenburgh. He leaned forward to pat his friend on the knee. "But all that is about to change. I am taking it upon myself to find you a suitable wife."

De Lacey regarded him with dawning horror, and stammered, "No, *mon ami*... There is no need... I do not wish..."

"It's quite obvious that you need to be pulled out of whatever doldrums you have let yourself fall into, my dear fellow. A wife with a good dowry will get you out of your current financial difficulties and may provide the very distraction you need, if she is pretty enough. And even if we are unable to locate you a wife, the process of doing so will provide quite a diversion." A smile split Lord Edenburgh's face, followed by a serious expression. "I'm quite worried about you, old fellow."

De Lacey smiled grimly. "You need not be, Quincey. I am capable of taking care of myself." He picked up his brandy glass and tipped it up, aware of the social faux pas of trying to drain the last drop from the already empty vessel but needing something on his tongue other than the sour taste of commitment.

"*Bien sûr*, I have considered taking a wife. It seems a most effective way to relieve me of my current difficulties—only what do I have to offer, Quincey? A worthless title and confiscated property? What woman would find those things enticing? Or rather, what woman's family?"

Lord Edenburgh waved his concerns away with a flourish. "Nonsense. We all know the situation in France will be resolved sooner or later and your titles and lands restored. Admittedly, it's taking longer than expected. But you're still confident, aren't you?"

"Of course." It was a lie. In the three years that De Lacey had been stranded in England, the French King and then the Queen were executed, and a reign of terror overtook France. Now, everything seemed to be teetering on a precipice. And while change was occurring, de Lacey could not see a place for himself in his country. Still, it was all he had left, so outwardly he clung to his title and the potential return of his property, even if he didn't feel it.

"Then all we need to do is secure a wife whose dowry will keep you until then. That will make the whole process much easier — we don't need to look for a girl with a sizeable fortune, just an acceptable one. You'll have dozens to choose from." Lord Edenburgh smiled at de Lacey, but he simply couldn't smile back. The thought of sifting through a mountain of debutantes was terrifying.

"*Mon ami*, I appreciate the assistance, I really do, only I think —"

"We start tomorrow, at the Grenville's ball."

"Tomorrow?"

"No time like the present, old fellow." Lord Edenburgh rubbed his hands together, and de Lacey was a little afraid of the gleeful look on his face. "We'll find you a suitable wife yet! Now, we should make a list." He patted his jacket pockets, looking for, de Lacey assumed, pencil and paper.

De Lacey looked around wildly, and caught the eye of the butler, who swiftly moved to his side.

"More brandy, Markham, *s'il vous plaît*. I'm going to need it."

CHAPTER TWO

Eugenie Ponnette stepped down from her carriage, her eyes lighting up at the spectacle of what seemed like hundreds of gentlemen and ladies converging on Lord Bullsbrook's stately home. There were carriages everywhere–large, imposing coaches with coats-of-arms on the doors, smaller but still meticulously shiny hired coaches, light and fast curricles, and then drivers for all these conveyances shouting for their right-of-way to either approach the house, or retreat from it.

The grand manor was ablaze with lights–intricate lamps stood in many sconces leading the way to the front steps which were strewn with produce, in keeping with the harvest theme. One couldn't take a step without treading on a squash vine or a string of beans. Fruit and vegetables that had found their way under the guests' feet made the steps treacherously slippery, and servants tried desperately to sweep the offending mess away, even as more guests arrived to track more of the morass into the receiving area.

Eugenie registered the smells of the fruit and vegetables, coupled with the general scent of the London street–oil in lamps, the tang of garbage, and horse dung (although the collectors had been quite vigilant knowing the street would be filled with people tonight, horses would be horses, and when there were so many of them in a small area, there could only be one outcome).

The smell inside was little better, coupled as it was with the overbearing heat. Eugenie was all but overcome by perfumes of pomade, hair tonics, scents and colognes mixed with that of unwashed heated bodies, spilled drinks and more of the harvest. Lush produce was artfully arranged in magnificent cornucopias that sat alongside white statuary depicting every Greek god from Apollo to Zeus. Lady Bullsbrook had certainly outdone herself.

Eugenie's eyes shone as she handed her cloak to a waiting servant and was ushered into a retiring room. Her favorite thing to do in Paris was dance, and this was her first real opportunity since arriving from France.

She had hesitated to come, unwilling to leave her poorly *maman*, and uncertain if she would be able to enjoy herself through the worry over her *papa*. But her *maman* had insisted, and now, Eugenie was very glad she had.

"Lady Underwood and Miss Eugenie Ponnette." The stentorian tones of the butler announced their names across the room as Eugenie was rewarded with her first glimpse of the ballroom itself.

"*Incroyable,*" Eugenie whispered to herself.

Dozens of couples danced a complicated quadrille while hundreds of other people lined the walls, watching. Eugenie knew that in other rooms, card tables would be available, along with areas where refreshments could be obtained. There was a supper room that would be opened later, as well as multiple double doors leading out to balconies and down into the gardens.

Lady Underwood took Eugenie's arm. "Come, my dear, it's unseemly to stare. You'll stick out like a country bumpkin." They strolled to where a crony of Lady Underwood's stood, and Lady Underwood engaged her in conversation. But Eugenie stayed silent, scanning the crowds for her best friend, Felicity.

There she was. Standing against the wall a little way away, dressed in a gown that had obviously been chosen by her mother, it was so ill-suited for her. Eugenie wanted to run to her and hug her; she looked so miserable. She was unlikely to be asked to dance except by a few who considered it a duty or a chore, and Felicity knew it.

Poor Lady Felicity Merryweather was red-headed and freckled. Despite treatments ranging from lemon to lead powder, her mother had failed to rid her of the hideous flaw. And at her mother's insistence, she still only wore debutante colors—the palest of pinks, blues, and yellows, which did nothing to improve her complexion. Eugenie knew Felicity would be better served by wearing stronger shades of blue, green, and purple, but Felicity would not gainsay her mother. Eugenie only hoped that there were some gentlemen in London prepared to look beyond the hideous gown and its less-than-fashionable coloring to see the lovely girl who resided beneath it.

She excused herself from her aunt's side as soon as it was polite to do so, and made her way over to Felicity, who fixed her with a baleful stare as she approached. Eugenie smiled encouragingly at her friend, whose grimace transformed into a genuine smile of friendship, elevating her plain features. When Felicity smiled, her pale blue eyes shone, and her fine white teeth showed between a lovely pair of sweet lips.

"*Mon amie*, please, you should smile all the time. You look beautiful when you smile," said Eugenie upon reaching her, taking her in her arms and kissing her on both cheeks, according to the French tradition. Felicity replied, "You are the first thing I've come across worth smiling at since I arrived."

"Nonsense. Look at the people! The dancing! It's beautiful." Eugenie eagerly scanned the crowd, hearing the music trill above the hum of conversation, and watching the dancers glide and spin as they executed the steps.

"It's surprising how the more you watch, and the less you engage in dancing, the less beautiful it becomes." Felicity sounded tired and dispirited, so Eugenie wound her arm around her friend's waist.

"Well, *mon amie*, here I am to make you more cheerful. Although I do have to warn you, if a gentleman does ask me to dance, I'm simply not sure that I could say no."

Felicity laughed—another of her wonderful features. "And I would smile, my dear, to see you dancing, for I know you love it so, and I know how much effort your mama undertook to encourage you to do that very thing. I certainly don't expect you to remain here all evening just to keep me company. I'm quite used to not being asked to dance. Are you attending Mama's little dinner on Thursday?"

"We had planned on it, yes."

"Good. It would be a great bore otherwise. Mama doesn't truly know how to host a little dinner party. I believe there will be upwards of five and thirty guests."

"Six and thirty, surely, to keep numbers even?" Eugenie's eyes twinkled, matched by the sparkle in Felicity's.

"Knowing Mama, that wouldn't even be a consideration. Goodness!"

Her rapid change of tone made Eugenie start. "What is it?"

"I've just spied an old family friend coming this way. He used to be plain old Viscount Healey, but since the death of his uncle and cousin, he has inherited the title Earl of Edenburgh."

Interested, Eugenie looked around, straining to discover which gentleman Felicity referred to. But since she was quite a bit shorter than Felicity, all she could see were the backs and heads of her fellow guests. "Which one is he?"

"Eugenie! It's not as if I can point at him."

"But *mon amie*! He may be the one to produce my grand passion!"

Felicity snorted. "I'd be very surprised if he produced a grand passion in you."

Eugenie had strong ideas about the gentleman she would eventually marry. Love was definitely in the cards. In fact, she insisted she would not marry when love was not in evidence. But there was no reason why she should not fall in love with an earl, or even a duke, if he produced a grand passion in her, was there?

"Perhaps you can turn your head and indicate the direction he is approaching from."

"Shh! He is right there."

Two gentlemen approached the ladies, and from his familiarity with Felicity, Eugenie realized that the shorter and more portly of the two was the aforementioned Earl of Edenburgh. Felicity was right. The gentleman would never inspire Eugenie to a grand passion. She sighed under her breath.

"Lady Felicity, it's been an age. How is your father?" The gentleman bowed over her hand, smiling what Eugenie thought was a genuine smile. Felicity, too, smiled her lovely smile back at the earl.

"He is very well, thank you. He misses seeing you at Merryweather House."

Eugenie realized that her initial impression that the earl was portly was not, in fact, justified. Stocky, certainly. But not portly. It was just that his friend was so tall and slender. Eugenie glanced at him as he observed the old friends greeting with a resigned expression on his admittedly handsome, though far too old, face.

She surmised he was on the wrong side of thirty, despite his good looks. His eyes were a lovely clear green, but the creases around his mouth, on his forehead and beside his eyes showed that he carried some worries. His dark hair, brushed fashionably, showed threads of gray. There was something familiar about the gentleman. This was not Eugenie's first party, so she may have seen him at some other event during the season.

The earl turned to Eugenie and said, "Lady Felicity, will you introduce me to your friend?" Eugenie curtseyed, then smiling, looked up again into the face of the friendly earl. He radiated warmth and invitation, like a chubby puppy that just wanted to sleep in your lap while you snuggled into a comfortable chair. Eugenie liked him immediately.

"My lord, this is Eugenie Ponnette, niece of Lady Underwood. Eugenie, this is Quincey, Earl of Edenburgh."

"Ah, Lady Underwood. Of course. I can see the resemblance. Charmed, I'm sure," replied the earl, bowing over the hand she offered. "French, then?"

"*Oui*," replied Eugenie.

"Visitor?"

"*Non. Émigré*, I am afraid."

The earl smiled. "As is my friend here. Ladies, may I introduce Vicomte Landreville."

"So, that is probably why you are familiar," Eugenie blurted out the words, before remembering her manners. She blushed. "*Excusez-moi*, monsieur. I have a terrible habit of saying whatever I am thinking."

"It is forgiven, mademoiselle," replied the vicomte without humor or any color in his voice. There was an awkward silence, eventually filled by the earl's hearty tones.

"Lady Felicity, may I have the honor of securing the next country dance? I do believe it is about to form." Felicity forced a smile and Eugenie sympathized with her friend, knowing that Felicity hated to feel as if she were an obligation. However, Felicity replied bravely, "It will be my pleasure, my lord."

"De Lacey, you should ask Mademoiselle Ponnette to dance as well. Then we can continue our conversation."

Eugenie glanced up at the vicomte to find him scowling at the earl, an expression he quickly hid as he turned to Eugenie. "May I have this dance, mademoiselle?" he asked in his polished English. It was with some reluctance that she replied, "Certainly, monsieur."

Eugenie took his arm, and he led her to the floor. Turning to face the vicomte, she regarded him with narrowed eyes from beneath her brows. He glanced at her disinterestedly, and then looked away, only for his eyes to immediately return to her face as he realized she was glowering at him. "Is something wrong, mademoiselle?" he asked.

Eugenie schooled her features into an innocent expression. "Why, no monsieur. Whatever gave you that idea?"

"Merely the fact that you were looking at me as if you wanted to *garotte* me, instead of dance with me." A half-smile formed on his face and Eugenie registered that the vicomte was very handsome indeed. However, that was neither here nor there.

"Oh, no. As a matter of fact, I was wondering exactly the opposite," she replied, starting the steps of the dance with a curtsey.

"Exactly opposite? Whether I wanted to *garotte* you instead of dance with you? I can assure you, mademoiselle, I have no desire to hasten the demise of such a lovely lady." Eugenie noted his

15

perfect execution of the dance steps, but that was only to be expected since he was French. She was much more interested in his face, where his brows had drawn together over his narrowed eyes, a glimmer of green regarding Eugenie lazily.

"I dislike being a chore, monsieur." Her tone was light, but she set her jaw and stared belligerently into the gentleman's face. "If you did not wish to dance with me, you should not have asked."

"And what leads you to believe I do not wish to dance with you?"

"I saw your face when Lord Edenburgh suggested it." She silently dared him to refute her words, but he didn't, only smiling at her as if he was an indulgent parent, and she a petulant child.

Well, if childish is what he wished for, then childish is what he would get.

"You are not enjoying the dance then?"

"No, I am not." Using the steps of the dance as a cover, she stomped on his toe with force. "Oh, dear. I do apologize, monsieur."

After a wince of pain, the vicomte chuckled. "Not at all, mademoiselle. I find that I am enjoying dancing with you more and more." Eugenie watched as his expression sharpened, his eyes focusing completely on her. "You are quite refreshing compared to some of the other young ladies."

"Refreshing?"

"Yes. You are certainly not the only young lady who has stood on my toes tonight, but I am sure you are the only one who has done it deliberately."

She smiled sweetly. "You might be surprised, monsieur. Perhaps they were just not so open about it as I."

"Ah, but you see, that is the charm."

"So, I am charming because I deliberately hurt you? That does not make any sense."

"You are right; it does not. But there it is." He regarded her speculatively for a moment then leaned into her, his voice quietly intimate. "Do you notice the malaise that clouds this city, mademoiselle? The insipidity?"

Eugenie drew back in surprise. "No, monsieur. I do not. Although I will admit the English are more concerned with reputation rather than etiquette, I don't find it affects my enjoyment at all."

"Well, you see, there we are different. I suppose I prefer the pretty manners and underlying intrigue of Paris. At least there I can exercise my wit."

"Indeed, monsieur, for it has been in short supply this evening."

He blinked, staring open mouthed at her for a moment, before throwing his head back and laughing. Couples alongside them tried to distance themselves from the unseemly noise, and Eugenie colored. "Monsieur! Please. You make a spectacle of us."

"And that is not what you sought when you stomped on my foot?" He drew her as close as propriety would allow, and stared down into her eyes, a rakish smile on his face and his eyes now a mocking dark moss green. Eugenie gasped.

"No! All I wanted was for my dancing partner to show some interest in me."

"And am I not doing so?"

"Far too much interest, monsieur." For some reason, Eugenie's heart was racing, and her mouth went dry. The vicomte was regarding her with a predatory stare, and for a heartbeat, Eugenie wished he would press his lips to hers, regardless of propriety and reputation. With the next heartbeat, the wanton thought was replaced with disquiet at the vicomte's proximity. His glance flicked back up to her alarmed visage, and he immediately let her go, the steps of the dance taking them away from each other for a few moments. Eugenie used the reprieve to slow her pulse and puzzle over the strange feelings that came over her when she was in the vicomte's arms.

When they re-engaged, the vicomte smiled wickedly. "I do hope your enjoyment of the dance has improved, mademoiselle. I know mine has. Immensely."

"You take too many liberties, monsieur," Eugenie loftily advised him.

"I am well aware," he replied in a tone of mournful remorse.

"You seem contrite, but I don't know if you are sincere or if you are mocking me."

"I'm mocking you, mademoiselle. For a certainty." Now, his eyes gleamed a bright, deep green. His amusement was palpable, and Eugenie was a little annoyed that he was taking his pleasure in trying to fluster her.

"You are no gentleman," she said scathingly.

"You need to be more careful what you wish for then mademoiselle. For dancing with a gentleman would certainly be less interesting than dancing with me."

Thankfully, for Eugenie at least, the dance ended just then, and the vicomte had no recourse other than to walk her back to her aunt's care. She strolled stiffly beside him, careful not to look at him, and ignoring the various amusing and scandalous comments that he made about the other guests in the ballroom. He seemed to be attempting to shock her, to elicit a look or a laugh, but Eugenie refused to give him the satisfaction.

They arrived beside Lady Underwood who smiled at the vicomte with confusion before addressing Eugenie a little waspishly. "My dear, I'm not sure that I am acquainted with your partner."

"This is Vicomte Landreville, Aunt. A fellow *émigré*."

"Ah, so this is the famous Landreville. It's lovely to meet you, vicomte," purred Lady Underwood, simpering over his offered hand. Eugenie, surprised that her aunt seemed to know of the vicomte, noticed him stiffen before he replied, "And you, my Lady."

"Did you enjoy your dance with our little Eugenie? Isn't she a treasure?" Eugenie frowned. There was some undercurrent to the conversation she did not understand.

"Actually, I enjoyed it significantly more than I expected to, madame." At Lady Underwood's confused expression, he turned to Eugenie. "Thank you for the dance, Mademoiselle Ponnette. It was a pleasure." He took her hand and placed a kiss on it, lingering for far longer than was seemly. A shock of electricity passed up her arm and down to her stomach, and Eugenie pulled her hand away in alarm. He walked away, chuckling to himself.

"What on earth was that about?" asked Lady Underwood.

Eugenie tried to slow her treacherous heart, that had beat quicker at the vicomte's touch. "He is an odious man," she said in a furious whisper to her aunt. "No morals, no propriety. He spent the entirety of the dance trying to discompose me."

"Really?" replied Aunt Lucinda, unfurling her fan with a flick and lazily fanning herself as she watched the viscount walk away. "How interesting."

De Lacey strolled back to where Lord Edenburgh had deposited Lady Felicity with her mother, a smile playing about his features.

"Well, de Lacey, that's the happiest I've seen you in months," said Lord Edenburgh.

"That may be so, Quincey. I actually discovered in amongst the thorns perhaps a rose. Or at least a debutante who is as clever as she is beautiful."

Lord Edenburgh grinned. "So, do we have a winner? Is the ever unattainable de Lacey looking at his future wife?"

Felicity and her mother gasped, their heads turning toward the two gentlemen. De Lacey colored and glared at his friend, grasping his elbow and turning him away from the curious women. "She is far too young. And an *émigré*."

"That is a problem?"

"She is probably every bit as impoverished as I am."

"Pity. She is quite lovely." Lord Edenburgh looked across the room. "You know she hasn't taken her eyes off you since you walked away from her?"

"I'm certain she is trying to turn me to ash with her glare," replied de Lacey with a chuckle. "We did not leave on good terms."

"No? What did you do?"

"I scandalized her with a kiss to the hand."

Lord Edenburgh chuckled. "My friend, you are incorrigible."

"My dear fellow, you have no idea." De Lacey glanced again across the room and found himself a little disappointed that Mademoiselle Ponnette's glare no longer rested on him. He had the strangest desire to return to her side, to say something that would return the smile to her face, the interested light to her eyes.

She was one to keep in mind.

CHAPTER THREE

Several long hours later, de Lacey let himself into his lodgings on Jermyn Street. The sharp odor of tallow candles was an unwelcome reminder of his penury, as was the uncomfortable chafing his unraveling shirt cuff caused against his wrist.

He untied his cravat and started to unwind it from his neck, his movement slowing as a thoughtful expression crossed his face. It had certainly been an instructive evening. He must have spoken with thirty women, most of them the vacuous, simpering fools he expected. However, the evening had also proven to him that amongst the irritating, flirtatious throng, he could potentially find a bride. The thought was somehow satisfying, even if the notion of being shackled to one woman for the rest of his days was decidedly distasteful.

De Lacey had met several ladies that evening who might suffice, but none that interested him as much as the *émigré* girl, Mademoiselle Ponnette. She intrigued him, with her scorn and her innocence. Knowing nothing about her was a gap in his knowledge he planned to fill almost immediately.

"Tatillion! Where are you, you scoundrel?"

His manservant minced into the room, immaculate despite the early hour. De Lacey idly wondered whether the man ever slept.

"Monsieur, why are you home? There are many hours left before you should be dragging your bones back to the door. I didn't brush your hair in the Brutus style and tie your cravat just so, for you to come home early."

"*Mon dieu*, Tatillion, stop complaining and help me with this blasted cravat."

With a tortured sigh, Tatillion approached de Lacey and took over the unwinding of the cravat, treating it as if it were a delicate object, instead of a length of muslin. For a moment, de Lacey was annoyed with his servant's finicky manner.

"And find me some brandy, will you?"

"*Certainemant*, monsieur. I have secured some fine French brandy — so much better than the pigswill these English call brandy, *n'est-ce pas*?"

"And just how do you know that? Been sampling the goods, have you?"

Tatillion affected shock. "*Moi*? I am crushed, monsieur, that you should even suggest such a thing." He helped de Lacey out of his coat and located the brandy, pouring a sizeable glass and offering it to his master.

De Lacey sat in a comfortable chair, sighing in relief as he did. "These London events will be the death of me. All manners and propriety, no intrigue, no excitement. Never anything special."

Tatillion sniffed, placing the bottle of brandy back on the sideboard. "The English could not throw a ball to save their souls. If only they had seen our beautiful salons and soirees in Paris. They would know not to keep trying. It only makes them look more stupid than they are."

De Lacey silently agreed before taking a sip of the brandy, which was very good indeed.

"Tatillion, I need you to find something out for me."

Tatillion's eyes shone. "Spying? Excellent. Is it for the French or the English?"

For a moment, de Lacey was confused, and then he realized Tatillion's meaning.

"No, I don't mean for the war."

"Oh."

"I need you to find out what you can about a certain Mademoiselle Eugenie Ponnette."

Tatillion's brows drew down. "Ponnette? Where have I heard

that name? Oh yes!" The servant's face brightened, and he clicked his fingers. "The mother and daughter émigrés. Very beautiful, I have heard."

"The daughter is lovely, to be sure, but I haven't yet met the mother."

Tatillion's eyebrow raised. "Are we pursuing this young lady, monsieur?"

"Pursuing?" De Lacey affected an innocent expression. "Whatever do you mean?"

"Your reputation precedes you, monsieur," replied Tatillion dryly. "Is she to be your next conquest? For you were usually not interested in young ladies. Had you said you were interested in the mother, then I might have understood."

De Lacey felt an unusual irritation at Tatillion's line of questioning.

"I am merely curious, that's all."

"Merely curious?"

"*Oui.*"

Tatillion was silent, his brow still raised. The silence ticked on between them, until it drove de Lacey to spurt, "Very well, I'm considering her for a suitable wife."

At this, Tatillion took a step back. "A wife?"

"*Oui.* I am in considerable financial difficulty, as you are well aware. The only recourse seems to be to find a wife. However, of course, she must have a reasonable dowry that will sustain our livelihood until such time as my lands and incomes are restored to me."

"Then your smuggler friends were not able to help with more funds?"

De Lacey sighed. Tatillion was privy to all his deepest, darkest secrets. Having first been his companion as a boy, and then his manservant when he grew, Tatillion had been by de Lacey's side through all his adventures. When de Lacey confided to Tatillion that he was making plans to secretly emigrate, Tatillion insisted on accompanying him, even when de Lacey advised it would be a hand-to-mouth existence. The fastidious Tatillion had shuddered but declared his intention to continue by his master's side.

Indeed, Tatillion was something of a mystery to de Lacey, even now. Slight and birdlike in his movements, Tatillion always looked as if he had stepped off a fashion plate, despite his second-hand clothes and his workload. He had a keen sense of style, to the extent that sometimes de Lacey would like to slap his hands away when he insisted upon adjusting a fold in a cravat for the tenth time.

But beneath his feminine-like exterior, Tatillion was quick with a pistol, skilled with his hands and feet, and had been able to talk de Lacey out of trouble on more than one occasion. His disdain for the English was legendary amongst de Lacey's friends and his loyalty to de Lacey priceless.

"It's more that they can't help with funds," replied de Lacey. "The London lifestyle costs more than they could ever dream of earning—and the proceeds from each transaction have to be shared between all of the operatives."

"Hmm," said Tatillion, his hands on his hips. "But, a wife? Are we certain this is the right thing to do?"

"Of course not. But it seems the only practical course of action."

"And this Mademoiselle Ponnette is a viable option?"

"I won't know until you find out what there is to know about her." De Lacey frowned and turned to his servant. "A viable option? She's not stocks and bonds."

"No indeed. In fact, she seems quite the popular heroine."

"What makes you say that?"

"She and her mother were caught up in the September massacres. Then, as they were fleeing, mademoiselle's maid was killed right at her side."

"Really?"

"Bullet in the back."

"How awful."

"Yet, mademoiselle kept her calm, and guided her mother out of the city, along with the other servants and all they could carry. Apparently, she orchestrated the whole thing."

"Interesting. Our Mademoiselle Ponnette becomes more and

more fascinating the more I learn about her. Do see what else you can find out, won't you, Tatillion?"

"*Certainement*, monsieur. I will make it my mission."

CHAPTER FOUR

The woman seated at the dressing table had her back to de Lacey, but from under lowered lashes she watched him in the glass, wandering about the room, picking up a picture here, an ornament there, but not really looking at anything, his distraction palpable. She shook a few drops of Olympian Dew onto her hands and rubbed them together, then moved them over her neck and down to her exposed decolletage, all the while watching for some response from her lover. There was none. Her peacock blue silken chemise, tied securely at the waist, splayed at her thighs, leaving her long, creamy legs in view; but even those, which would usually have de Lacey's devout attention, failed to interest him. There was obviously something on his mind.

She would not ask. He would tell her when he was ready.

Shrugging to her reflection, she stood and glided to him, draping her arms around him and placing her chin on his shoulder. He was just the right height for her to lean against—tall and slender, with hard muscle where necessary. She was taller than what was fashionable, but she felt that was why de Lacey had been attracted to her in the first place. That, and her dark red hair. He had made it plain that her hair was his favorite feature. She wore it loose now, cascading down her back in shining, russet waves.

She placed a kiss on his cheek. "Jean. Come to bed."

He chuckled softly. "You are insatiable, madame." He rested one of his hands on hers.

She pouted. "I haven't seen you in almost a week."

"Is that how long it's been? I hadn't noticed."

She playfully slapped him, and stepped away, only to have de Lacey pull her back into his arms and kiss her with a passion that made her quiver from head to toe. She deepened the kiss, and he responded by winding his hands into her hair.

"*Ma chérie*, I know how long it has been to the minute," he breathed. She smiled through his kisses.

But to her disappointment, he let her go before their lovemaking heightened and wandered over to the cabinet to pour himself a brandy. He indicated with the bottle and one raised eyebrow to ask if she wanted one; she shook her head no. She sat back in the dressing table chair turning it away from the mirror and into the boudoir.

De Lacey hesitated, lowering his glass from his lips and setting it back on the top of the cabinet. Then, he turned to face her.

"I'm thinking about getting married."

Ah, there it was. "Congratulations. Who is the fortunate lady?"

"There are several possibilities, but I am leaning toward one. Her name is Eugenie Ponnette."

The woman thought for a moment, then shook her head. "I can't say that I know of her." She stood and drew near to him, kissing his cheek. "Congratulations, darling. I wish you well." Then she paused for a moment, pulling the top of her chemise closed. "You know, I might need that drink after all." Pouring a large measure, she drank the spirit in one gulp, slightly annoyed by the look of amusement on de Lacey's face as she did.

She asked, "What is it that draws you to this particular lady?"

De Lacey waved a hand in the air, almost as if he was brushing away an annoying insect. "She is beautiful and has money, and doesn't seem too irritating." He, too, finished his drink. She took the glass from him and filled it again.

"Are you certain, then?"

"About what? Marriage?"

"That they are the only characteristics that you are seeking?"

"Of course. There are no other considerations required. It's not as if it will be a love match."

She smiled gently, taking his face in her hands. "Then you should not marry her, Jean." The surprise on his face was unmistakable, and she continued. "My darling, you of all people should find yourself a love match. You have so much passion to give."

"I spend my passion with you, *ma chérie*. My wife will be an amusing companion, will make a good mother to my children, and bring enough money so that we will not suffer the indignity of having to beg on the streets."

"Did it cross your mind that your wife may not like the thought of you having a lover?"

De Lacey raised one eyebrow and said in a haughty tone, "Does her opinion really count in the matter?"

She laughed at his naivety. "Oh Jean, you're adorable. Of course her opinion will matter. She may not have many rights as a married woman, but she can certainly organize to avoid your bed if she knows you are sleeping with other women."

"She cannot deny me my marital rights!"

De Lacey seemed outraged by her words, and she gurgled in delight at his ignorance. "Oh, but she can, darling. Perhaps not outright, but we women have our tricks. She could make your life a misery."

"But I don't want to let you go because of this." He swept her into his arms. "You remind me so much of Celeste, *ma chérie*. I'm not ready to let go of that particular memory."

It saddened her a little. She knew de Lacey didn't love her, just the woman she reminded him of. She didn't know any of the details, apart from that she was a French woman, and he had lost her. "Perhaps we need to let go of our memories of lost love to move ahead with our lives," she replied.

"Well, I don't wish to." De Lacey pouted like a sulky child, and she smoothed his hair back and kissed his forehead.

"Poor darling," she crooned. "It's never fair when life insists on a path that takes us away from our natural inclinations."

"I've hardly been a one-woman man."

"I know."

"Surely nobody expects me to change my basest nature."

"Marriage has been known to change a man, my dear."

"I have needs." He pulled her close, and she felt his not insignificant manhood rub up against her thigh.

"As does every man in England. And I'm sure your wife would meet those needs admirably if you loved her."

"Stop it." He looked her squarely in the eye. "I don't wish to discuss it further."

She shrugged. "Whatever you say, darling." His eyes drifted toward her decolletage, darkening with passion. She smiled and took the two sides of her chemise in her hands, opening the garment and giving him access to her smooth breasts. His lips followed where his eyes landed, and she let her head fall back. If nothing else, she would have de Lacey for tonight.

CHAPTER FIVE

To de Lacey's dismay, the soiree at the Lovelace's house was overrun with people. He had hoped that by choosing a smaller party to attend he might have some space to breathe; but while there were fewer guests, there was also a much smaller space to hold them all.

It was only a short while into the season, and already he felt overwhelmed. He was sure that in Paris, there had never been such an attraction for squeezing the greatest number of people into the smallest possible area. London hostesses vied for the title of Crush of the Season as if it were a mantle of honor. A crush was a marker of success. De Lacey didn't understand it at all.

He stood to the side of the room, champagne in hand, beside Lord Lovelace, who had lamented that his house had been all but ransacked by his wife to create a space to hold the soiree. Lord Lovelace, an accomplished politician, accepted the necessity of his home being invaded by strangers from time to time, but even he seemed irritated by the crowds. Lord Lovelace's white mustache seemed to bristle with indignation.

"Mark my words, Landreville, if she ever again asks to hold a soiree, I will say unequivocally, no. I spend the whole day in session at parliament and I don't need my home, where I come to relax and unwind in the bosom of my family, overrun by all kinds of wastrels and hangers-on who have no care for my welfare, and who are only here to empty my liquor cabinet and my coffers."

Since Lady Lovelace was a known and accomplished hostess, de

Lacey rightly assumed Lord Lovelace was just letting off some steam, so he let the gentleman talk, affecting interest in his conversation while scanning the crowds for a more entertaining companion. Preferably female.

With relief, he spotted Mademoiselle Ponnette at the other side of the room. Now would be as good a time as any to familiarize himself with the little French woman. She was the clear front runner, in de Lacey's mind, for his hand. So long as she didn't turn out to be a shrew. Or a dreadful bore. Or Tatillion discovered she was a pauper.

De Lacey interrupted Lord Lovelace's tirade, his hands held in front of him as if praying. "Monsieur, I do apologize, only, there is a beautiful woman on the other side of the room that I particularly wish to know better. Will you not excuse me?"

Lord Lovelace huffed at him through his mustache, but grumbled, "Go ahead, young man. I suppose no young buck would really be interested in talking to an old windbag like me when there are eligible ladies present."

Bowing, de Lacey made his escape.

He was on his way across the room to Eugenie's side when, to his surprise, he heard her voice, shrill above the crowds.

"You will not speak of her in such a way!"

There was a momentary hush in the room as the guests looked around to see who had made the outburst but the conversational buzz was soon restored.

Reaching her side, de Lacey was surprised to find her color high, and a group of three young men surrounding her, the scent of brandy strong in the air. The men were so young—only boys, really—and de Lacey wondered if this was their first brush with the effects of strong spirits. One of the lads, a short, dark haired fellow, took Eugenie's hand, which she snatched away. Another, also dark but tall, snaked an arm around her waist. The third, a thin red headed youth, blocked her path, one finger raised as if admonishing her. He seemed to be attempting to say something very serious to her. However, his words were slurred as he stumbled toward her. She jerked backward which only put her

31

closer to the other two louts. She looked affronted and aggrieved, and very, very lovely.

"Gentlemen."

De Lacey's single word gave the youths pause, enough for Eugenie to scuttle over and stand slightly behind de Lacey, her hand gripped tight around his upper arm. De Lacey caught the fear in her expression and felt a rising anger at the three drunk reprobates. He stood straighter and faced them. Having a tall, older gentleman get between them and their quarry seemed to disarm the trio.

"You're not her father, are you?" De Lacey raised an eyebrow, feeling a little discomfited that they thought him that old. At two-and-thirty he had been sowing his wild oats for quite a few years, but certainly, he could not be old enough to be Mademoiselle Ponnette's father. He fixed them with a fierce stare.

"I am not. However, I cannot stand by and watch you accost this young woman and disgrace yourselves in such a way." The three colored and hung their heads. The tall, dark one murmured mutinously, "It was just a little fun."

"A little fun? The young woman is scared witless." At Eugenie's outraged gasp, de Lacey patted the hand that was still tight around his upper arm.

"I am not scared witless," she said in a scandalized whisper. "I had the situation under control."

"Scared witless," he said again, emphasizing each word. Eugenie slapped him. The youth's heads dropped lower, eyes fixed to the floor. "You should offer the young lady your most sincere apologies, and then take yourselves home to sleep off the brandy." He drew Eugenie around to stand in front of him and pointed to the tall, dark youth. "You first."

The young man took a sheepish step forward, glanced up into Eugenie's face, and said, "I am truly sorry, miss. It will not happen again."

Like clockwork, the other two came forward in their turn and offered their apologies. Eugenie took it all with a set jaw and fire burning in her eyes.

32

As the third youth stepped back, de Lacey said, "Now go, before I track down your fathers and divulge what you have been up to."

Fear flashed across the countenances of the young men, as they took to their heels. De Lacey watched them exit the room, and then he turned back to Eugenie.

Despite her bravado, now in the aftermath, de Lacey could see angry fearful tears close to the surface. He took her by the arm and murmured, "Come, let us get some air."

Eugenie allowed him to lead her out on to a terrace, where a slight breeze blew the scent of frangipani and jasmine toward them. Eugenie leaned on the balcony, and a great sob seized her.

To de Lacey's surprise a strong feeling of protectiveness toward Eugenie pulsed inside. He wanted nothing more than to take her in his arms, to kiss her tears away, to whisper silly nothings to her until she regained her equanimity. But for once he allowed propriety to guide his actions. He only placed a hand on her arm. "Are you alright, mademoiselle?" He drew his handkerchief from inside his coat and handed it to her.

"I shall be, presently," she replied, taking the offered handkerchief and dabbing her eyes dry. "It's just the shock, that's all."

"What happened?" De Lacey tucked the handkerchief back into his pocket.

Eugenie's eyes fired. "They were disparaging Felicity, saying that she was ugly and awkward when she is no such thing. I had no choice but to defend her."

"Of course." De Lacey could imagine the spirited little minx jumping to her friend's defense, even if it meant pitting her petite, feminine self against three drunken louts. He only wished he had reached her side in time enough to spare her their unwelcome attentions.

She continued, "I am not even sure they heard what I said. They encircled me and said how lovely I was. I took no notice of their nonsense, and tried to ignore them, tried to get away. But one of them grabbed my wrist."

"It is poor form, even when one is in his cups, to mishandle a lady."

She caught and kept his eye. "I could have taken care of myself, you know."

"I know. You are renowned at fending for yourself. But I am relieved that you didn't have to."

She frowned. "Why did you say that?"

"What?"

"That I'm renowned at fending for myself?"

"Merely gossip, my dear. It seems you are lauded as somewhat of a heroine for your escape from Paris."

She shook her head, her shoulders slumping. "No. I was no heroine. There was nothing heroic about our escape."

De Lacey sighed, leaning his back against the balcony beside her. "Nor mine. Is it not funny? The English think it must have been so romantic and daring, but I…" He stopped and swallowed, not willing to delve too deeply into his feelings.

"You feel as though you are a fraud?" She smiled wryly. "That would seem to be something we have in common, monsieur." She was silent for a moment before adding, "Did you leave anyone over there? Family? Or friends?"

His thoughts skipped to Celeste. "Yes," he replied shortly.

"My *papa* is still there, and it breaks my heart to think of it. He was imprisoned. And I am terrified for his safety." Her head dipped. "I find it difficult to be merry when I know he is in such straits."

He turned his head to look at her. "I am glad we have found something we agree on, mademoiselle," de Lacey replied gravely.

Eugenie smiled gently. "As am I." She put a tentative hand on his sleeve and looked up into his face. "Thank you for coming to my rescue, monsieur. I do appreciate it."

De Lacey found himself staring into her lovely face with its dewy, blue eyes, and porcelain complexion, and he colored like a callow schoolboy. His mouth went dry, and he was seized by a strong desire to kiss her. His eyes alighted on her rosebud lips, and his breathing became a little erratic. Yes, Eugenie Ponnette was a lovely woman. But his emotions seemed excessive for the circumstances in which he found himself. He had lusted after women before, but this was something else, something different. He couldn't even speak to her, his power of speech seemed to be suspended, as the air between them sizzled with crackling energy. He stopped breathing altogether.

And then Eugenie blinked and the moment passed. De Lacey moved restlessly, a long sigh escaping him. What on earth had come over him? He gave himself a little shake, and stood up, offering his arm to Eugenie. "Shall we return to the ballroom, mademoiselle? I do believe I hear the musicians striking up a lively reel."

She placed her hand on his arm, rewarding him with a blinding smile. "Thank you, monsieur. I should like that very much."

CHAPTER SIX

Despair hung like a blanket of fog over Eugenie as she walked the streets of Paris. The sans-culottes, drunk on the blood of their enemies, had returned to their houses to celebrate their victories and to sleep off their triumphs, leaving the birds to pick over the bodies, even as the people had picked over them earlier.

However, now the birds were silent. The heavy quiet was broken only by Eugenie's footfalls against the uneven cobblestones.

She walked without direction, knowing somehow that if she made a decision, she would only regret it. She pulled her cloak tightly around herself, shivering in what felt like the early morning air. Her wandering footsteps took her to the Rue de Vaugirard, outside the prison that used to be the Carmelite Convent. Large brown stains on the steps of the prison and the metallic tang in the air told a story of blood and massacre.

She blinked, now finding herself at the Abbaye Prison, which, too, was dark and cold. A glint of sunlight bounced off a drinking glass, and Eugenie was horrified to discover it appeared to contain remnants of blood. The cobblestones here still ran with the blood of those slain, discarded axes and saws showing the darkening remains of their thirsty work.

She heard a woman's scream, blinked again, and found herself at the Place Dauphin, a roaring fire belting out heat into the dawn. To her horror, the remains of at least a dozen people lay strewn about, blackened by the fire. A discarded bonnet lay just out of reach of the flames, crushed beyond saving, and one poor soul's body hung precariously off Pont Neuf.

Eugenie spun in fear at the touch of a hand on her shoulder, only to be confronted by a group of sans-culottes. They were dirty and blood-spattered, their eyes dead and their expressions slack. They held sabers, axes, and clubs, but all were close-mouthed, staring at Eugenie.

She started to back away, but the sans-culottes stepped with her. She choked back a sob, and turned to flee, only after a few terrifying steps she, too, was on the edge of the Pont Neuf. She turned back to the silent mob, but they were advancing on her.

The front most man thrust his sword in the air and cried, "Death to Aristocrats!"

But as he lunged and swung his sword, Eugenie jumped into the cold waters of the Seine.

With a scream, Eugenie awoke, drenched in perspiration. Her heart pounded, and her eyes searched the room, coming to light on her mother, who was seated beside her.

"Shh, *ma chérie*, you've had a nightmare," her mother soothed.

She threw herself into her mother's arms. "It was terrible, *maman*," she sobbed. "At all of the prisons, there was torture and massacre and so much blood."

"I know, *chérie* I know. But it was all a dream, *non*? We are here in London, with the massacres far behind us."

"But we still don't know if *papa* is alive, *maman*. How can you say it is behind us?"

A shadow crossed her mother's face, before she replied, "We pray, *ma chérie*. That's all we can do. We pray. And grieve those we have lost."

Eugenie slumped back on her bed. "It is the agony of not knowing that is the hardest, *maman*."

"I know, *ma chérie*. Her mother smoothed her hair and kissed her forehead. "Try to go back to sleep."

But Eugenie knew that sleep would be impossible to achieve for the remainder of the night.

CHAPTER SEVEN

De Lacey waited impatiently for the morning hours to pass before it was proper to call. Tatillion had seemed enraptured when de Lacey had requested the manservant dress him properly, although Tatillion bemoaned the state of his master's one presentable morning suit. However, the little man had worked wonders, first with de Lacey's cravat, as snowy white and crisp as that of the most fashionable gentleman, and then with his hair, face, and hands, which were manicured to perfection.

While he worked, Tatillion filled de Lacey in on the details he had unearthed about Mademoiselle Ponnette's family.

"Maurice Ponnette is the twelfth Baron, monsieur. The family is old and wealthy and royalist to the core." De Lacey couldn't tell how Tatillion felt about this snippet. De Lacey himself was hardly a royalist—society saw him as quite bourgeoisie since he chose to work despite his elevation to vicomte. Even so, he strongly opposed the forced return of his lands and titles to the state, and it was his outspokenness on this issue that had him driven out of France.

"His wife, Anselle, is the sister to the current Lady Underwood. I do believe that puts Mademoiselle Ponnette a little below you in station, monsieur."

De Lacey frowned. Tatillion was telling him nothing he didn't already know. He was a little nervous that his rank, despite being higher than Eugenie's fathers', would be disparaged because of its recency. He had only achieved the rank in the few years prior to the uprising.

"Go on," he urged. Tatillion tilted de Lacey's head back a little so he could work on the cravat.

"Their lands and titles were, of course, forfeited to the state, as were ours." At this, de Lacey's eyebrows raised, and Tatillion flushed. "Excuse me, I mean *yours*, however when restored, Mademoiselle Ponnette will be quite the heiress."

Yet another reason she might refuse him. His stomach tightened.

"Thank you, Tatillion, that will be enough for today."

The fastidious manservant's face fell. "But I have so much more to tell you. At least let me say, she would make you a suitable wife."

A smile played over de Lacey's face. Yes, she would. And he was most interested. Oh, a love match it would never be. She was far too young and impetuous to fall in love with. His tastes led to a much older and more experienced type of woman.

But she would certainly be interesting to live with, and he could imagine himself waking up to her lovely face each morning.

There was, however, one detail still to be discerned. "Her dowry. Tatillion, did you find out anything about that?"

Tatillion nodded, his shoulders straightening as he rushed to provide de Lacey with the details. "They did manage to bring some money by way of transferable stocks and bond certificates, and apart from that, Lady Underwood has convinced the duke to underwrite mademoiselle's dowry until such time as it is released by the French authorities."

"So, the amount?"

"A little over twelve thousand I believe, monsieur."

"Hmm, not a huge fortune, but certainly enough to go along on for a while, if the situation in France remains impossible."

"That was my understanding, monsieur."

"Good, good. Tatillion, you have outdone yourself."

The manservant preened a little under the approbation of his master.

"Now, hand me into my cloak, I must get going."

Arriving at Underwood House, where Madame Ponnette and her daughter were staying with their relatives, de Lacey was greeted with a flurry of activity.

"Don't let her outside!"

A black and white cat streaked past the door and down the stairs to what de Lacey assumed was the kitchen. The next streak was Mademoiselle Ponnette herself, who hesitated long enough to drop de Lacey a tiny curtsey and a breathless, "How do you do, vicomte?" before following the cat down the steps.

For a moment de Lacey stood, mouth open and eyes wide in surprise. Color crawled into his face at the sight of her tumbling curls, the pale green morning gown that clung to her ripe, young figure, and her flushed features, with the words falling from her full, cherry lips as she dashed past. He realized a moment of desire for the young woman—oh, to be permitted to lay his hands on those curves, to place kisses on those lips and down the porcelain column of her throat. He shivered just a little at the images in his mind.

De Lacey was shaken out of his reverie by the return of mademoiselle, happily carrying the large cat, who was now contentedly purring in her arms, though with large yellow eyes it looked askance at him as Mademoiselle Ponnette approached.

"Isabeau sometimes gets a little scared of the noise here in London," she said, flushing a little. The color was becoming. "I have to placate her. I do not usually run around the house like that."

"No, I'm sure," replied de Lacey cordially, swallowing his unwelcome feelings of attraction. It would not do to desire her.

"She came with us from France. I would not leave her behind." She sounded a little belligerent as if she was challenging him to disagree.

"That was very charitable of you, mademoiselle," he replied, then reached out to tickle the cat under the chin. She responded by stretching her neck and rumbling a loud purr.

Mademoiselle Ponnette seemed delighted. "She likes you, monsieur. That is approbation indeed, for she is quite particular about whom she likes."

"I do seem to have an affinity with the feline population," admitted de Lacey. "I am not certain why, but cats seem to like me." He tried to stop petting Isabeau, but she extended a paw and batted at him to continue, which he did.

Mademoiselle Ponnette laughed in delight. "Come, monsieur, we must go through to the morning room. My aunt and mother are there finishing breakfast."

De Lacey was at once cautious. "I do apologize, mademoiselle. Have I arrived too early?"

"Oh, no, monsieur. It is they who take breakfast far too late. We have another caller as well this morning—Mrs. Wilberforce is here."

Since he had no idea who the lady was, de Lacey said, "Well, in that case, let us make our way to the morning room at once."

The hum of conversation from the morning room floated down the hallway, becoming louder and more clear as they neared.

An unfamiliar voice said, "My dear, he is so handsome, and such a reputation. If I weren't happily married to my Charles, I should certainly set my cap at him."

"That is Mrs. Wilberforce," whispered Mademoiselle Ponnette. "She is the worst gossip in all of London. Mama likes to have her here because Mrs. Wilberforce fills her in on all the news."

"Set your cap?" a second voice said, which de Lacey recognised as Lady Underwood. "Why, my dear, he does not seek marriage. He is a scoundrel, apparently, who likes to keep discreet company with widows, and sometimes, married women as well."

"I wonder of whom it is they speak?" Mademoiselle Ponnette whispered to him, even as de Lacey's stomach was dropping.

His suspicions were confirmed when the butler introduced him, and all three ladies in the room swiveled around, shock on their faces. But Lady Underwood, well used to the social graces, was quick to recover.

"Vicomte Landreville. What a lovely surprise. And you found our little Eugenie as well." She smiled fondly at him, holding out her hand for him to kiss. He strode in and offered the expected greeting before Lady Underwood introduced the other ladies in the room.

"May I introduce Mrs. Wilberforce and Madame Ponnette." He nodded to each of the ladies in turn, significantly more interested in Madame Ponnette than in the other woman, who at a glance seemed to be the classic sharp-featured, stick thin, overdressed caricature of a gossipmonger.

He could see Eugenie's beauty reflected in her mother, though in the mother it was a faded beauty. She wore a lavender gown, and most of her golden curls were covered with a matching beribboned cap. An untouched cup of tea lay before her on the table.

He bowed to Mrs. Wilberforce, but took Madame Ponnette's hand and kissed it. She bestowed a gentle yet forced smile on him, as if finding the energy to smile was almost too much for her. "Please do be seated, vicomte," she said quietly, her voice a slightly deeper version of Eugenie's musical tones.

He noticed that Eugenie had taken a seat on a settee that was designed for two people, so he deposited himself beside her. Mrs. Wilberforce's eyes narrowed, but de Lacey did not care. Let her gossip. He was going to offer for Mademoiselle Ponnette soon enough.

Eugenie had pulled the cat into her lap, and de Lacey reached over to tickle Isabeau under the chin, which narrowed Mrs. Wilberforce's eyes even more. Belatedly realising how familiar the action would seem, he blushed and withdrew his hand. Isabeau, however, was having none of that. She stepped from Eugenie's lap to de Lacey's, and then sat staring up at him until he patted her.

"The cat seems to like you." Mrs. Wilberforce's tone made it clear she thought the cat was welcoming a friend. De Lacey rushed to disabuse her mind of the thought. "Indeed, which is very odd, since this is the first time I have been inside this house. It seems I have a kind of affinity with cats."

He knew he sounded like a gauche schoolboy, trying to cover up a mistake he had made, and he straightened, pushing the cat off his lap as he did so. Isabeau, disdaining such treatment from a mere human, sauntered out of the room, head held high and tail swishing.

"I felt obliged to call on Mademoiselle Ponnette after the incident last night," he started but paused when Eugenie threw him a glance and a very slight shake of the head.

"Incident?" Her mother was immediately attentive, reaching out a hand toward Eugenie. "What incident was that? Eugenie, you didn't tell us about any incident?"

"It was nothing, *maman*," replied Eugenie soothingly, with a glance of reproach at de Lacey.

"Well, it was certainly something since a gentleman has come to call today to ensure your health," Lady Underwood piped up, with an irritating titter.

Eugenie turned scarlet under her aunt's teasing, and de Lacey replied smoothly, "Nothing of the sort, Lady Underwood. Mademoiselle Ponnette merely defended her friend from some slightly inebriated young bucks at a soiree yesterday, and I came to her rescue when they decided to make some sport of her."

"Some sport?"

"They were teasing me, *maman*," Eugenie let out an exasperated sigh. "That's all. The vicomte was kind enough to rescue me from nothing and his concern for my wellbeing, no matter how kind, is misplaced in the extreme."

An awkward silence fell. It seemed that the room's occupants were reflecting on their own thoughts. Each face de Lacey glanced at showed a different emotion—Mademoiselle Ponnette was chagrined, her mother concerned, Lady Underwood looked at him from under her lashes, and Mrs. Wilberforce regarded him openly and boldly. He flushed under their inspection.

Mrs. Wilberforce broke the silence. "I must be going," she said, standing up in a smooth motion. "I promised Amelia Hartshorn that I would drop in this morning, and I have a hundred other things to do this afternoon, I simply can not imagine how I will manage them all."

Everyone stood, de Lacey executing a bow and Eugenie a

curtsey. After a quick clasp of Madame Ponnette's limp hand, Mrs. Wilberforce strolled to the exit, trailed by Lady Underwood.

The remaining women sat down again, followed by de Lacey. "I am sorry, mademoiselle, if I embarrassed you," he whispered, to which she answered, "It is of no consequence, monsieur. I merely didn't wish to make a fuss." He nodded, then addressed Madame Ponnette. "Will we see you out and about during the season at all Madame?" He flashed her a smile. "It seems a pity to shroud such beauty."

Despite the thin smile she returned, Madame replied, "I hope to attend a few small events at the very end of the season. However, I am so tired and heartsick; it is difficult to find the energy."

"If there is any service I can provide for you, madame, please do let me know," he said, glad that he could hear the genuine note in his own voice.

"I thank you, monsieur, however, according to my physician, all that is needed is rest and quiet. Would you like some tea?"

De Lacey accepted, and Madame Ponnette said, "Eugenie, would you be so kind as to pour a cup for the vicomte?"

Eugenie dutifully picked up the teapot and poured de Lacey a cup, handing it to him with a grave look on her face, and a sparkle in her eyes. De Lacey wondered just what was going on inside that mind of hers. She returned to sit beside the vicomte.

"Are you really here just to inquire after my health?"

De Lacey chuckled. "Indeed, I am; although I'm terrified to do so now. I fear it might prompt your fearsome feline to attack me."

Eugenie smiled. "Maybe a few minutes ago, but you should be safe now. I am quite alright, monsieur, following the incident."

"Ah, but you did have a nightmare last night, *mon cœur*," her mother said, disregarding the warning look that Eugenie sent her.

"Nightmare?"

After a moment's silence, Eugenie said, "I have some residual nightmares from our flight from Paris, usually brought on by situations of some distress."

"I suspect you aren't the only one, mademoiselle. It was a traumatic experience for many of us."

The statement hung unanswered in the air for a moment until Eugenie turned to de Lacey.

"Are you attending Countess Kenyon's musicale next week? It is said she will be presenting one of the foremost sopranos from Italy."

"I will have to check my invitations—I will admit, I do not usually attend musicales, but if you are likely to be in attendance, perhaps I will reconsider my stance against them." In his peripheral vision, de Lacey saw Madame Ponnette roll her eyes, then regard her daughter with a fond smile.

"You do not like music?"

"On the contrary, it is merely the soprano voice that I am not fond of. Sadly, it is also what most of the musical ladies in London prefer."

"True," she reflected. "It would be charming to hear a nice baritone or tenor from time to time."

"Ah," replied de Lacey with a cheeky grin. "But I suspect you ladies would do less listening and more ogling if that were the case."

Feigning an air of sincerity, Eugenie sighed. "It's true. Obviously, that's why the ladies continue to bring us sopranos."

"Obviously."

Isabeau deigned to strut back into the room. Apparently having forgiven de Lacey for his earlier error of judgment, she jumped straight onto his lap and curled up. He chuckled, stroked her soft fur, and was rewarded with a loud purr.

Eugenie shook her head in amazement. "I have never seen Isabeau take to someone quite the way she has taken to you, monsieur."

He grinned. "It is my magnetic personality and charming good looks."

"That must be it," Eugenie replied flatly, with a twinkle in her eye.

"However, poor Isabeau is to be disturbed again, since I should take my leave."

"So soon?" De Lacey was pleased to see Eugenie seemed

genuinely disappointed, as did her mother.

"We would be happy for you to visit longer, vicomte," Madame Ponnette said, and de Lacey bestowed another of his charming smiles on her.

"It is not *de rigeur* to stay above fifteen minutes, and I believe I have already outstayed my welcome. Besides, I am not sure I wish to arm Mrs. Wilberforce with even more ammunition."

Eugenie's mother smiled. "Dear Mrs. Wilberforce. She is certainly a font of information. For example, monsieur, she told me all about your flight from France."

"Did she?" De Lacey was at once interested and wary. Just what kind of story was being bandied around London about him? Some of the details were certainly not salubrious and certainly wouldn't assist in his pursuit of Mademoiselle Ponnette.

"Indeed. Rowing across the Channel in the black of night? It sounded very exciting to me."

"It was cold and wet and uncomfortable, madame," de Lacey replied, "and it is not something I should wish to do again soon."

Madame Ponnette nodded. "I do believe the English like to romanticize our journeys. I hear mine and Eugenie's was extremely exciting as well."

De Lacey laughed. "Indeed, madame, that is what I have heard." As Lady Underwood returned to the room, he said again, "I am about to take my leave, my lady. Do send my compliments to your husband, won't you?"

Lady Underwood seemed crestfallen. "So soon, monsieur? But you have only just arrived."

"Nevertheless, it is time to go." De Lacey was pleased to see Eugenie looked despondent as well. "I shall probably see you again at Countess Kenyon's musicale."

"I shall look forward to it," the young woman said gravely, standing and lifting the black and white cat from his lap. The cat seemed unperturbed, laying her front paws over Eugenie's slight shoulder and purring contentedly as Eugenie hugged her.

De Lacey also stood, and leaned over Eugenie for just a moment, whispering so only she could hear, "I wish I were that

46

cat."

With a laugh at her shocked expression, De Lacey took his leave.

CHAPTER EIGHT

Two evenings later, de Lacey dropped into a chair, letting all the breath out of his lungs, before lifting his tankard and clinking it against the full tankards of the other men around the table in a noisy, messy "Cheers!" They all took a hefty draught before slamming the tankards on the table and laughing together.

Only de Lacey couldn't laugh; he could only manage a wry smile. Tonight, he would have to tell the gang that he was done. And he was not looking forward to the exercise.

The drop had gone without a hitch, as usual. Not that it could have gone any other way, de Lacey reflected. Even if the excisemen appeared, they were outnumbered five to one. And the beaters in the Waldershare Gang could be brutal if required. De Lacey would hate to have to face them on a dark night.

"God love you, gents. Fine brandy, and at 'alf the price I'd usually pay!" The smile on the face of Thomas Finchley, the tavern keeper, stretched from one end to the other as he slapped the backs of the closest smugglers. De Lacey had heard Thomas was a pious and law-abiding citizen; however, he wasn't above taking on a little contraband if it became available.

"So long as you don't double the price back to us, Thomas!" The smugglers snorted with laughter, and Thomas joined in. The smugglers knew they would always be treated well at The Ancient Crow Inn.

"Aye, nor try to sell us tea instead of whiskey!" Another bellow of laughter filled the tavern, to which de Lacey added his small smile. Their cache this time had included both brandy and tea, along with smaller amounts of gin and coffee.

"De Lacey, what's up with you? You got a face like a wet blanket." Seated beside de Lacey, Arthur Gladstone elbowed him hard in the gut. "We just brought a ton of tea and a hutch full of spirits up the beach, man. Today, we be kings!" Again, tankards clinked, and drinks were downed.

After taking a fortifying drink himself, de Lacey decided to plunge right in. "I have to get out, Arthur."

The table went quiet. The men's expressions became shuttered and hardened. "You know it's not possible, lad." Arthur's voice held a note of warning, and de Lacey could feel the menace radiating off the other men at the table.

"You know I'm no threat. But I have to go straight."

"We are going straight, lad. It's them excisemen that're the criminals."

Arthur's words garnered a chorus of "too right," and "thieving bastards." But the voices were constrained, waiting to hear what de Lacey would say next.

"I need access to more funds than I can make through smuggling."

"Then do something extra on the side. But you won't be leaving the gang, Frenchie. You belong to us."

At this, de Lacey stood and slammed a hand down on the table. "I belong to no man but myself." Several others rose too, their hands reaching for their weapons, but Arthur waved them down as de Lacey continued. "Everywhere I go, someone wants to own me—la Revolution, l'English—well, I won't have it." He took a deep breath, and in a quieter voice he continued, "I have paid my debt to you."

Arthur raised one gray, shaggy eyebrow. "Do you think so, lad? Well, I think different." His voice held a note of threat and the air thickened between de Lacey and Arthur as they faced off.

But before things could escalate further, de Lacey was distracted by a flurry of skirts, and a rough feminine voice said, "You lads aren't robblin' again are you?"

Maggie, the innkeeper's daughter, settled herself in de Lacey's lap, and he was sure she wiggled her bottom in an effort to get a rise out of him. He smiled and whispered in her ear, "You are a very naughty girl, you know that?" His hands settled around her hips, and she threw one arm across his shoulders.

Arthur gave a sharp wave of his hand. "We'll talk about this later, lad. Jus' you and me. But for now," he held his tankard in the air, "death to the excise and long live the smugglers!" The roar of agreement signaled the end of hostilities with the other gang members, but de Lacey could see the hard eyes of the wily smuggler staring at him over the rim of his tankard.

Three hours later, de Lacey stumbled out of the inn, very much the worse for drink. The men had continued filling his tankard long after he had protested that he needed to return to London. Quick horses could get there in a day, and de Lacey was expected at Countess Kenyon's musicale the following night.

He stumbled to the stables, far too drunk to notice he was being followed.

"So, you want to get out, do you Frenchie?"

The soft voice came from behind him, and de Lacey spun unsteadily. Three men had followed him out of the bar, and even in his foggy state, he could see they held clubs. He knew he was in trouble.

They set upon him from all sides. The first man hit him across his back, and when de Lacey lurched forward from the blow, a second slammed him in the stomach with a club. He doubled over, trying to steady himself. However, pain and the effects of too much whiskey took their toll and he tumbled to the ground. The thugs continued to strike him with clubs and feet as he tried desperately to shield his head from their raining blows. He heard a crack, and a sharp pain sprung up in his wrist. He swore in his native tongue, cradling his damaged hand. The blows continued, and de Lacey curled up into a ball, wondering how long it would take to die. He prepared to be beaten to death until he heard a familiar voice say, "Enough."

With his vision blurring from the pain, de Lacey hardly noticed his head being yanked back and Arthur saying in his slack face, "You don't get to hetch away, lad." Then he was dropped to the ground, and the thugs walked away, their footsteps crunching on the inn's gravel driveway, their coarse laughter quickly dispersing into the night air.

The next thing he remembered was being dragged back into the inn, pushed into a chair, and someone holding him upright as Maggie and her mother swam in and out of his vision, clucking their tongues at his injuries, and scolding him.

"You couldn't keep your big gob shut, could you? Now look what's happened, you addle-headed man. Of course they pounced you. What did you expect?" But despite her scolding, Maggie tended his many cuts and bruises, smoothing the hair off his face, and kissing his forehead. "It looks like they been instructed not to bash you in the face. Lucky for you."

"I love you, Maggie," he slurred, and she bestowed a sweet smile on him.

"And I you, you stupid bastard."

"None of that now." Maggie's mother bustled back into the room. "I've made up a bed for you, do you think you can make it upstairs if you lean on Jack and Maggie?"

De Lacey nodded, but even that small movement had his head lolling, so Maggie and Jack more carried than assisted him up the stairs and into bed. He shut his eyes and groaned when his back hit the mattress, feeling every last one of his bruises, and the jarring in his wrist.

"We'll fetch the leech to look at that wrist for you, Jean, but you have to keep it still." Mrs. Finchley's words came to him through a fog of pain, and he moved the wrist to rest atop his ribs to stabilize it. Jack left the room in the hope of finding the doctor, and Mrs. Finchley followed him.

Opening his eyes again, de Lacey felt Maggie's curls tickle his face as she straightened the bedclothes around him. Despite his exhaustion, drunkenness, and pain, he smiled as seductively as he could manage and said, "Why don't you stay, Maggie?"

"With you? Stinkin' to high heaven, drunk as a sailor and broke into a thousand pieces?"

"There are parts of me that are not broken." He tried to lift his hips a little, and a groan escaped him.

"Now't but I reckon that part might be broken too." Her tone softened. "At least if you're thinkin' o'that you can't be too badly injured, so that's a relief. I was worrit for you when I seed those men doggin' you. I love you, you know. So, so much." She dropped a kiss on his forehead, and he let his eyes close again with a worried sigh.

Maggie had told him she loved him more than once and that she would gladly marry him. It was a conversation they had had before, and even through his pain and alcoholic fog, de Lacey knew he needed to make the situation clear to Maggie.

He reached out his good hand to her. "Maggie, you know I cannot marry you, *hein*? No matter how much you think you love me." He caught her gaze and her sudden frown of anger.

"No, I do not. You're not a high and mighty noble here, you know. Just a man. You don't need to keep up your play act of bein' a somebody. You already are a somebody. To me." Her voice was swallowed up by her tears, and de Lacey drew her close enough so that she could sit beside him on the bed.

"But I am a vicomte, *chérie*. And in France, we take our nobility very seriously."

"Aye, and just look where that got you." Her tone had turned mocking. "Thrawn out of your own country, penniless and friendless. You're just lucky Arthur and the lads took you in at all. And they've been good to you, haven't they?"

De Lacey nodded, the movement making his head ache. The gang had been good to him. They had given him passage on the condition that he organize their cargo of silks and lace on the French side. De Lacey had always attracted plenty of women and had always treated his ladies well, so he had insider knowledge of the trade in Paris and the surrounding countryside. This knowledge enabled him to secure a sizeable cargo for the boat, which turned his friends a good profit on the other side of the channel.

The smugglers had landed at a little sheltered cove they had known about on the coast between Hythe and Folkestone. They had remarked on his distress at being cast out of his own country and assisted the poor bewildered de Lacey to the town of Ashford, where he could easily secure conveyance to London. Then they had given him part of the profits from the deal.

"Yes, *chérie*, they have been good to me. Of course they have. But three years have passed, and I had expected to be free of them by now." Proving himself so valuable to the smugglers had been a mistake. They had since charged him with all kinds of duties on their behalf, from receiving goods in London and peddling them to the various known retailers, through to writing to his contacts in France regarding more and more merchandise. Heaven knew what would happen if one of his letters were intercepted. He suspected he would be thrown out of England before he could even pack a bag. He couldn't return to France, so where would he go? Italy perhaps? Or maybe America?

"And free of me?" Her plaintive tone caused him to peer into her eyes. He smiled and indicated she should lie in the crook of his good arm, which she did with alacrity. He kissed her temple, and she snuggled in closer to him. After the evening she'd had, it was no surprise to de Lacey that her eyelids fluttered down and shortly, her breathing deepened. She was asleep.

He would have to sort this thing out with Maggie eventually. No matter how much she had convinced herself, he would never marry her. But how on earth could he convince her of that?

CHAPTER NINE

She waited for him in the boudoir, artistically and provocatively draped over one of her Louis XIV chaises, only, when he came in, she could see his bruised and battered body was in no shape for lovemaking.

"Whatever have you done to yourself de Lacey?" she exclaimed. "Why, your body is covered in bruises. And your wrist is bound!"

She leaped up and assisted him to her chaise, and he relaxed into it with a pained sigh, even as he said, "I am fine. However, I could use a brandy."

"Of course," she replied, hurrying to pour him a large measure. Crossing back over the floor she handed the drink to him, asking, "Is there anything else I can get you? A compress? Or something from the apothecary?"

He smiled, and she could see the affection in his face. He liked her to be hovering over him. "I'll be alright in a few days, *ma chérie*. I just met with a little accident while I was away."

"What kind of an accident?" She sat across from him on a brocade chair, making sure the edges of her dressing gown crossed primly below the knee. It wouldn't do to entice him—not with his body in that state.

"A coaching accident."

She raised one eyebrow. She had seen injuries from being flung around in a coach, and what de Lacey sported was nothing like that. For one thing, his face was unmarked which, had he been inside a coach when it fell, would certainly not be the case.

His reasons for not telling her the truth were, of course, his own concern. She had no business prying, so she went along with his lie, shaking her head and saying, "Those coaches are a death trap. You so often hear about them breaking down and tipping over. Was anyone else hurt?"

"Yes, a few others, but they sustained only minor injuries—bruises and contusions."

"You must have been at the bottom of the pile, the number of bruises I can see."

He smiled and said, "Wait until you see them all." With that, he removed his jacket, cravat, and shirt. She could see every movement pained him, but she knew intuitively that her assistance would not be appreciated. When he removed his shirt, she gasped.

"Jean! Your ribs! Oh, my dear, they are just one enormous bruise."

He gave a wry smile. "I'm proud to say, I cushioned several ladies. Could you do me a small favor, *chérie*?"

"Of course. What do you need?"

He shifted uncomfortably on the chaise. "In my jacket pocket, there is a salve. Would you be so kind as to apply some to the worst of the bruising?"

"Certainly," she replied and moved with alacrity to where he had dropped his coat on the floor. Fishing in the inside pocket, she found the little jar of salve, which contained a strong numbing ingredient. She generously applied the salve to his chest, arms and back, one moment reveling in the feel of hard muscle under his smooth skin, and the next, hesitating each time he winced. It was obvious to her that he had been kicked or beaten. She wondered what had happened to him, and wished a little forlornly that their relationship was such that he would confide in her.

Somehow, that reminded her of his search for a wife.

"How does it fare with wooing your little French bride?"

Ah, here was a topic de Lacey seemed glad to expound upon. She watched his face light up. "We have had several conversations, and I am more and more pleased with her. She is clever and entertaining."

"Clever and entertaining." She echoed his words, raising one fine eyebrow. "Is that all?"

De Lacey colored. "What else should there be?"

"Love? Affection?"

He smiled. "I have already told you, it is not going to be a love match."

"Well, then affection at the very least?"

"Very well, if you insist, yes, there are some small tendrils of affection developing."

She rewarded him with a smile. "That's all I ask for, my dear. I want to see you happily married, not just settling for the best of a bad bunch."

De Lacey frowned. "There is one other matter I need to settle, though, before I can marry."

Her stomach dropped. This was where he would tell her it was over between them. She put on a brave face, knowing it would have ended sooner or later. Pushing impartiality into her tone, she said, "Oh? What is that?"

"Well, you see, there is this young woman on the coast."

"Dear me." Her relief that it wasn't the end of their relationship gave way to a tug of jealousy for the girl from the coast. He had another lover? Just how many women did one man need?

"Yes. I do not believe I have ever given her any indication thereof, but she seems to have it planted firmly in her head that I am likely to marry her."

"Goodness. What are you going to do?"

"That is what I wanted to ask you. How shall I let the young woman down gently?"

She moved to sit close beside him on the chaise. "My dear, no matter how you let her down, it is not going to be gentle if she thinks you are going to marry her."

De Lacey's shoulders slumped. "That is what I was afraid of."

"All you can do is be brutally honest with her. There is no easy way to tear a woman's heart from her body."

De Lacey growled under his breath and finished his brandy. "Tear her heart from her body? I fear you endow her with too much sensibility. Heaven knows why I ever got involved with her."

"I think I can work out why," she replied wryly, and a twinkle appeared in de Lacey's eye.

"Well, when it is offered freely, how can any red-blooded man resist?"

"Surely the circumstances you find yourself in right now should give you reason enough," she replied pertly.

He gave a small, self-deprecating smile. "You are right, of course, but I do find it particularly difficult to resist."

"You have much love to give, Jean."

He turned his head to her and raised one eyebrow. "You truly believe this is about love?"

She waved one hand impatiently. "Love, lust—whatever you choose to name it, you suffer from an excess of it."

"That I do. Although," he turned to lean his back against the side of the chaise, and lifted his feet on to her lap, "right now, I could not think of anything I should like to do less. My body aches like the very devil."

"You are welcome to stay, of course," she replied, "I shall ensure you remain undisturbed. However, I do believe you would be more comfortable lying down. Shall I help you to the bed?"

He accepted her assistance and moments later, he drifted off into slumber. She watched him for a long moment, before stroking his cheek gently. "Oh, Jean, what am I to do with you?"

CHAPTER TEN

"Did you enjoy Signora Bellissini's performance?" the earl asked politely, handing both Eugenie and Felicity a glass of orgeat. Eugenie lowered her eyes to take a sip—and to avoid having to answer the question. Signora Bellissini was said to be one of the foremost sopranos in Italy. However, Eugenie had not heard a single note.

Now, listening to Lord Edenburgh and Felicity discussing Signora's mellifluous tones, she was sorry she had devoted the time to listen out for any sound that might suggest Vicomte Landreville had entered, and then, upon the slightest inference, craning her neck to look for him. She felt ridiculous and irritated to know that her head could be turned by one scandalous sentence uttered at the end of what was a wholly un-scandalous morning visit. Yet here she was, moping because he hadn't arrived at the musicale when he said he would.

The word of such a man could never be taken seriously; she knew that. So why had she been so excited at the thought of seeing him here? And why was she so disappointed that he hadn't come?

"Eugenie? What did you think of Signora Bellissini's interpretation of the *Il Seraglio* piece?"

Eugenie blinked back to her present company and flushed at finding two pairs of inquisitive eyes staring back at her. "I beg your pardon; what was the question?"

"The *Il Seraglio* aria, Eugenie. Did you enjoy Signora Belissini's interpretation of it?"

The way Felicity couched the question, and the way both she and the earl were looking at her expectantly, she assumed her answer was supposed to settle a question between them.

"I... did not like it?"

"You see?" Felicity turned on Lord Edenburgh triumphantly. "Eugenie didn't like it either. Far too much trilling around in the higher register, don't you think, Eugenie?"

"Yes, certainly. Far too much trilling."

The earl bowed, his eyes dancing. "Far be it for me to defy the opinion of two such learned ladies. I consider myself humbly educated in the intricacies of the high register."

Felicity seemed highly satisfied by the earl's remark. "As well you might," she replied with an air of loftiness, "since we are so obviously the superior intellect in this matter."

"Now, now, Lady Felicity, I would not go quite that far."

Eugenie had to smile. When Felicity and Lord Edenburgh forgot their due consequence, and just bantered like a pair of old friends, Felicity shone. It was during these times that Eugenie thought Felicity her most beautiful, and hoped others could see it too.

However, her shine was not to last. A sultry voice from behind Eugenie said, "My Lord Edenburgh, Lady Felicity, it is lovely to see you both again."

Felicity immediately shrunk back, even as Lord Edenburgh eagerly turned toward the voice.

"Lady Hampshire, a pleasure, as always," he said, bowing over her hand. "May I introduce Mademoiselle Eugenie Ponnette? She is recently arrived from the continent."

"So, you are Mademoiselle Ponnette? I have heard much about you."

Curtseying to the lady, Eugenie couldn't help but notice—Lady Hampshire was luminously beautiful. And she immediately realized why Felicity had blanched—Lady Hampshire had lovely dark red hair and unblemished porcelain skin. She was the perfect version of the pale English beauty that Felicity, by way of powders and concoctions, tried to be. Of course, Lady Hampshire wore a stunning gown of dark blue sarcenet over a silver tissue underlay, a gown which accentuated her womanly features, while Felicity wore a pale jonquil silk gown, flounced in all the wrong places, that only made her look angular and sallow. Beside Lady Hampshire, Felicity became the wallflower she was said to be.

Eugenie's heart went out to her friend, but of course, Lady Hampshire was not to blame, so Eugenie pasted a pleasant expression on her face.

"Good evening, Lady Hampshire. It is lovely to make your acquaintance."

"Have you enjoyed the evening, mademoiselle?" The question was innocent; still, Eugenie blushed, thinking of her lack of attention. "Very much so. Signora Bellissini's voice was lovely, don't you think?"

Lady Hampshire looked around furtively, then leaned in to whisper to Eugenie, "In truth, I didn't hear a note of it. I'm not terribly enamored of the soprano voice."

Without thinking, Eugenie replied, "Similar to Vicomte Landreville, then?"

"Who?"

Eugenie colored, flustered at having given away the direction of her thoughts.

"Vicomte Landreville. He is a good friend of Lord Edenburgh's." The earl nodded, although Eugenie noted his wickedly shining eyes.

Lady Hampshire's eyes narrowed. "Vicomte...? Oh, certainly, the tall Frenchman? With the graying sideburns?"

"*Oui*, that is he."

"I'm not sure I'm acquainted with your vicomte. Is he here tonight?" She looked around as Eugenie wished for the floor to open and swallow her. Both Felicity and Lord Edenburgh were standing back, smiling broadly at Eugenie's discomfort. Such good friends as they were!

"Oh, no, you are mistaken, my lady. He is not *my* vicomte. He is merely an acquaintance." Lady Hampshire's sharp gaze return to Eugenie's face.

"Interesting. And yet you noted his absence."

"He specifically mentioned that he would be here tonight." Nervously, Eugenie smoothed the skirt of her dress and tucked a strand of hair back behind her ear. She shot an entreating look to Lord Edenburgh and Felicity to rescue her.

"He said he would be here, did he? That's surprising since he usually shuns musicales as if they were his own funeral." Lord Edenburgh smiled innocently at Eugenie, who scowled at him. He wasn't helping.

"In this instance, he said he might attend."

Lady Hampshire laughed, a flutelike trill that caused Eugenie's flush to deepen. She patted Eugenie's arm.

"We understand, mademoiselle. Come, my lord, stop teasing the poor girl. Now, mademoiselle, tell me, how much truth can we expect from the stories of your exit from Paris?"

Eugenie replied, "Very little, my lady, from what I've heard."

"So, you didn't singlehandedly rescue your entire family?"

For a moment, Eugenie's heart hurt. "No, my lady. My father is still there, in the clutches of the *Montagnards*." The Mountain was the most radical group in the National Assembly, responsible for the reign of terror and the massacres. Eugenie shivered, despite the heat of the room.

Lady Hampshire lowered her voice and replied, "I do apologize, mademoiselle. I did not realize you suffered still. Let us talk of something else." Eugenie threw her a grateful look. "Have you seen the Misses Granger? Their new French modiste has managed to mangle every single style she has put her hand to." She pointed out a pair of young women across the room whose gowns, while of fashionable colors, were a mix of a number of different styles which did not flatter the styles or the ladies.

"Is that a round gown dressed to look *a la Turque*?" asked Eugenie with a grimace.

"I believe so. Isn't it hideous?" Behind her fan, Lady Hampshire said, "I have the feeling that their modiste may very well have a thick cockney accent rather than a French one." Then she jumped a little. "Oh dear. There's Lady Kellerman. I meant to speak to her earlier, and then completely forgot. You'll excuse me, won't you? It was charming to meet you, mademoiselle. My lord, Lady Felicity."

"And you, my lady."

In a flutter of dark blue and silver, Lady Hampshire departed, and Eugenie felt as if a whirlwind had just passed. She turned to Lord Edenburgh.

"You!" she said in mock accusation. "You were supposed to rescue me."

His expression was nothing but innocence. "I have not the inkling of an idea of that which you speak of, mademoiselle."

He was goading her; she could tell by the amused sparkle in his eye, however, before she could gird up a reply, he sobered, and said, "I will admit to a little concern if de Lacey said he would be here. One thing he is not is a man to break his word. And especially not when it is made to a lovely young woman."

"That's exactly what I thought," replied Eugenie. "Had he no intention of attending, I would not have expected he would speak of the matter at all."

"When did he speak of the matter to you, mademoiselle?"

"Several days ago, he paid a morning call and mentioned he might attend."

"A morning call? De Lacey?"

"De Lacey?"

At Eugenie's furrowed brow, the earl explained, "It is the vicomte's surname. Jean Marie Natale de Lacey, Vicomte Landreville."

"Ah." Eugenie's brow cleared a little, then furrowed again. "Is it such a surprise, my lord? Certainly, the vicomte is accustomed to paying morning calls when the occasion warrants it?"

The earl regarded her shrewdly now. "And the occasion warranted it?"

"Yes. I ran into a spot of bother with some young bucks at a soiree we both attended, and the vicomte was kind enough to offer me assistance."

"And the morning call?"

"Was to console himself that I had suffered no ill from the encounter."

While it hadn't really struck her at the time, Eugenie was frowning now. Was it the behavior of a disinterested acquaintance? Or did the vicomte's conduct speak of some other, more personal attention?

Then again, he had not attended the musicale.

Confirmed in her own mind, Eugenie continued. "It was merely a nice gesture from a friend. That is all."

Lord Edenburgh's brow raised, but he nodded in agreement. "A nice gesture indeed."

"He meant nothing by it."

"I suggested no such thing."

"The expression on your face suggests it."

"Mademoiselle, I can assure you, the expression on my face is caused merely by concern over my friend."

"If you insist."

Felicity, who hadn't appeared to have paid attention to Eugenie and Lord Edenburgh's bickering, said, "She is a much nicer person than I would have thought such a beautiful woman to be."

"Yes, she is lovely," replied the earl, a faraway look in his eyes.

"I meant her personality is lovely, Quincey," replied Felicity, shaking her head and smiling at her friend.

As they bantered, Eugenie's thoughts turned back to the vicomte. Indeed, no matter how hard she tried, she could not keep her thoughts from returning to him, despite her disgust at herself for such churlish behavior.

Lord Edenburgh seemed concerned that he had not attended the musicale. Should she also be concerned?

Should she be feeling anything at all where the vicomte was concerned?

CHAPTER ELEVEN

De Lacey tried to keep his eyes open to stop himself from swaying on his feet. While it was not unusual for gentlemen to accept invitations and then fob them off when a better offer came along, de Lacey felt quite dismayed that he had missed Countess Kenyon's musicale. The fact that he had been laid up in bed recovering after having his wrist manipulated by a quack surgeon, whom he was certain had done more harm than good, was beside the point.

So, he had attended the very next ball he could, despite Tatillion scolding him and insisting he should stay in bed until at least the pallor had left his face. He really was in quite a bit of pain, the salve working effectively on his bruises, but not on his damaged wrist. He reached for another glass of wine, remembering this time to be sure not to use his injured wrist. That had been a mistake that very nearly cost him his dignity. Thankfully, there had been a convenient chair for him to fall into until the light-headedness had passed.

He had been searching for Mademoiselle Ponnette, of course, so he could apologize for his absence at the musicale. He had met Quincey at the club the day before, who informed him of the conversation he'd had with Eugenie.

"She seems quite taken with you, de Lacey," the earl had said, examining de Lacey's reactions. "She was quite chagrined that you were not there. Especially since you had particularly mentioned it to her when you called on her."

"Indeed, Mademoiselle Ponnette is an interesting young woman," de Lacey replied, trying hard not to give away his real thoughts on the matter. As it was, they were jumbled beyond recognition. It was not like de Lacey to vacillate over a woman. One charmed them, bedded them, enjoyed their company, and when the relationship started to wear down, one let them down gently. It was a method he had employed time and time again.

However, this time, it was marriage he was seeking. And while it was proving quite an easy task to charm Mademoiselle Ponnette, he realized this was a decision of which he had to be completely sure. After all, he would be connected to her forever, should he decide to marry her.

"You seem quite reflective over there," said the earl. "Are you in love with her?"

"Good God, no," de Lacey shot back, even as a little voice in his head asked, *are you?*

"No," he emphasized. "She is all that is lovely and beautiful, and she is fascinating to speak with and not at all like a dull debutante, but I am not in love. Me? Quincey?"

"Methinks the gentleman doth protest too much," said the earl, a twinkle in his kindly brown eyes.

"And methinks the earl is putting too much stock in what is obviously a fig of his imagination," retorted de Lacey.

"Figment."

"*Excusez-moi?*"

"Figment of your imagination. Not a fig."

De Lacey had scowled at him.

But now, here at the ball, scanning the crowds for that very same young woman, de Lacey wondered. Was he in love? It certainly felt different from his previous conquests. He felt the need to shelter Eugenie, to make her laugh, to be beside her. Celeste had not wanted his protection, had not needed it. And he found he quite liked the sensation of being needed.

His absence hadn't dulled his feelings either, which was a surprise. And being unable to find her was filling him with concern. Maybe she wasn't going to attend this particular ball. Ah, but Quincey had told him that she was, even though he hadn't asked, and Quincey somehow seemed to know everything about everyone.

Ah! Finally, there she was, coming through the doorway in a shimmering pale green gown that showcased her radiant blonde beauty. He felt at once proud and possessive that such a lovely woman might possibly be his. He started across the room, oblivious to the amused glances that he drew.

As Eugenie caught his eye, she smiled radiantly, then a look of chagrin crossed her features, and she frowned. De Lacey assumed she had recalled that he had left her high and dry at the musicale. He threw every ounce of his considerable charm into his smile, and, as he reached her, he bade a quick good evening to her aunt, and then turned to Eugenie. Taking her unwillingly outstretched hand, he planned to grace her ears with a beautiful speech explaining why he hadn't attended the musicale. However, he had forgotten again—that was his injured wrist.

The world spun, and his vision grayed around the edges. He heard Eugenie say, "Dear me, monsieur, are you quite well?" before experiencing the vague feeling he was being steered toward a seat. The room was sweltering and the crowd around him suffocating. Eugenie sat beside him and fanned him, while Lady Underwood on the other side chafed his hand. Thankfully, she was chafing the opposite wrist, otherwise, he probably would have passed out altogether. Someone handed him a glass of wine, and he sipped it, allowing the cool beverage to trickle down his throat.

After a few moments, he had recovered sufficiently to say weakly, "Thank you, mademoiselle, madame. You see, I injured my wrist a few days ago, and I'm still getting used to..."

"Shh," Eugenie said, still fanning him. "You're still a terrible color." Then her tone changed to one of gentle chastisement. "What made you come out tonight when you are obviously so ill? It was quite foolish of you." Despite his fuzziness and growing embarrassment, he found himself charmed by her concern.

He turned his head toward her aunt. "Lady Underwood, thank

you for not allowing me to make a spectacle of myself."

"Nonsense," replied Eugenie's aunt. "If we can't help our fellow man when he is in need, what good are we as human beings?" His regard for the older woman raised a few notches.

He took a few deep breaths, and the room returned to its usual colors and temperature.

"Thank you, my ladies. I appear to be adequately recovered. Now, may I relieve you of my presence? I do believe that together we have created quite a scene." He knew, and he suspected Eugenie's aunt would know as well, that the scene would be played out in many morning rooms across the city tomorrow, as well as in the society pages. It wasn't every day a vicomte passed out into the arms of a beautiful lady. He didn't wish for Eugenie to garner more attention than she already had.

But Eugenie was having nothing of it. "That is hardly the most pressing matter. You should be taking yourself home immediately, monsieur. You are obviously in no state to be socializing."

De Lacey was almost fully recovered now, and his wicked sense of humor reasserted itself. "On the contrary, I can not think of a better state to be in. I'm surrounded by two beautiful ladies whose only concern is my health. It's almost paradise."

Lady Underwood smiled in genuine amusement, while Eugenie giggled. De Lacey took to his feet gingerly, preparing for his head to swim. Thankfully, it didn't. "Perhaps to show my gratitude, you would each favor me with a dance?"

Lady Underwood stood. "I for one am far too fatigued to dance tonight. However, I do thank you for the offer, vicomte. Come, Eugenie. I need to find a beverage after all that excitement. Don't even think about offering to fetch them for us, vicomte. You couldn't carry them, not with your wrist. You'd end up pitching them to the floor."

Eugenie was slower to rise and looked into de Lacey's face. "I…" She started, then de Lacey noticed an expression of resolve cross her features. "I should very much like to dance with you, monsieur. The Quadrille?"

A smile crossed his face. "I look forward to it, mademoiselle." He bowed and walked away from them.

Quincey approached him. "Good God, de Lacey, you certainly do go to all kinds of lengths to win your lady's hand, don't you?" He laughed. "The betting books will be full of it tomorrow morning."

"Betting books?"

"Yes, about when you and Mademoiselle Ponnette will tie the knot."

De Lacey sighed. He'd forgotten about the cherished English pastime of wagering on anything and everything. He'd managed to do nothing but embroil his beloved in scandal.

Beloved?

Even as his head tried to work out what his heart already seemed to know, a servant approached them. The servant bowed to de Lacey. "Monsieur, there is a note for you." He handed de Lacey the wafer, bowed, and disappeared.

"Oh, a note? An assignation, perhaps?"

De Lacey opened the note and grimaced.

"An assignation, but not one I particularly wanted."

"My dear fellow, don't keep me in such suspense. Which lady seeks your undivided attention? Mademoiselle Ponnette has not had time to write you a note, so it must be your mysterious lover."

A half smile crossed his face as he regarded his friend's almost puppy-like excitement. "I'm sorry to disappoint you, my friend. It's a business transaction."

"Oh." The disappointment on Quincey's face was laughable.

Eugenie was radiant. She stood beside Felicity, who today was dressed in a hideous shade of very light puce with far too much lace and far too much fabric.

"I do believe Monsieur de Lacey favors me, *mon amie*," she confided to Felicity. Her twinkling eyes followed him as he spoke to the Earl of Edenburgh, and they narrowed as he read the missive he received.

Felicity, too, noticed him receive the note. "Perhaps he is too wicked for you, Eugenie?" She said with a troubled look on her face. "If he is receiving notes and making assignations, is that the kind of man you would wish to marry?" She looked around furtively, then lifted her fan to her face. "I've heard he has a lover."

Eugenie, too, was troubled. The studied casualness of receiving the note and tucking it into his sleeve seemed to suggest a liaison she didn't like to think of. And if, as Felicity said, he had a lover, that would create even more problems. She could never have her grand passion with a man who would keep a mistress in addition to a wife.

"I have to see whom he meets," whispered Eugenie into Felicity's ear. Felicity was shocked. "You can't do that! You'll expose yourself to as much scandal as whomever he might meet."

"Not if I keep myself well hidden. I just want to see who it is," Eugenie insisted. "And if it is someone I disapprove of, I'll approach them and berate him."

Felicity paled and almost begged Eugenie to stay beside her when she noticed the twinkle in Eugenie's eyes. "You are cruel," she said. "I thought you were serious."

"About approaching them? Not at all. But about spying? I couldn't be more serious."

She kept her eye on de Lacey, and when he casually looked around and then slipped out through an open door to the garden, she followed, being as circumspect as she could.

CHAPTER TWELVE

Rounding a quiet corner of the garden, she followed to within earshot of de Lacey's voice, hiding herself in a hedge as best she could. To her surprise, he seemed to be conversing with a servant, and a male servant at that. Certainly not a romantic assignation. Eugenie sighed a relieved sigh. She really wasn't sure what she would have done if she had come across him in the grip of a tryst.

Then, she listened in on what de Lacey and the other man were saying.

"I said I was out."

The suppressed fury in de Lacey's voice came as an unwelcome surprise to Eugenie. She gasped, her dress accidentally rustling the hedges around her hiding place. Eyes widening in alarm, she held her breath and hoped her slight movement hadn't been detected. To her relief, the men seemed too engrossed in their conversation to notice a little hedge-rustling.

"Don't bark at me, Jean. You knew what you were getting into."

"I did not expect indefinite servitude."

"No?" The man's soft chuckle sounded sinister.

"No. So you go back, and you tell them I won't be coming."

"Tell 'em yourself. I'm just the messenger."

Eugenie's sharp ears heard footsteps that disappeared into the night, and she assumed the servant—if, in fact, that was what he was—had gone. She could hear her quarry pacing around the grass, muttering ferocious oaths to himself under his breath in French. She was glad she didn't hear most of them—the ones she could hear were certainly never meant for a lady's ears.

Then he let out a great sigh, and said in a slightly louder voice, "You may come out now Mademoiselle Ponnette."

Cold settled over her like a blanket and the color drained from her face. For a split second, she hoped he was talking to some other Mademoiselle Ponnette who just happened to be hidden in the bushes. But no. The gentleman knew she was there.

Eugenie's pulse pounded in her head, but she set her face in the most composed expression she could manage and stepped daintily out of the bushes as if it were an everyday occurrence for a young lady to do so. She tugged her pale green gown free of the prickly hedge and winced when the lace ripped. Eugenie put one hand up to pat her hair, seeking foreign objects, and thankfully, did not find any. Then, she turned to face the vicomte.

The gentleman looked her up and down, and sighed again, before turning away.

"*Attendez!* Wait!" She took a step toward him, reaching out to touch his sleeve. He looked down to her white-gloved hand against the forest green of his evening coat, as did she.

When he looked up into her eyes again, his smoldering expression alarmed her. She tried to take a step back, but he captured her, pulling her into his arms, his lips finding hers. At first, she struggled, but the novelty of his hard body and the giddy sensation of his lips molded against hers, worked their way into her consciousness, and she stilled, giving in to the delicious decadence of the kiss.

The vicomte was not a gentle lover. He kept one arm locked around Eugenie's waist; his other grasped her jaw. He worked his lips over hers, and Eugenie felt the roughness of his stubble against the fine skin of her face. It tantalized her, this minor knowledge of the differences between man and woman. He pushed his tongue against Eugenie's lips and, surprised, she opened her mouth a little. That was all the invitation the vicomte needed. His tongue invaded her mouth, engaging her in a battle she could never win. She felt a fluttering in her lower abdomen, something fierce and primal that she had never felt before, but that she instinctively knew could be tamed by the vicomte's touch. She pushed herself hard up against him, whimpering her need.

With yet another muttered oath, he pushed her away. Eugenie noticed his drawn brows and harsh breathing. He pulled at his cravat and swallowed before saying, "Let that be a lesson to you, mademoiselle. Terrible things happen to young ladies who eavesdrop."

"I didn't think it so very terrible."

Her eyes widened, and a blush started from the very soles of her feet up to the top of her head. Who ever thought she would say something so audacious! She held her head a little higher as de Lacey's brows raised in surprise, and an unexpected chuckle escaped him.

"Neither did I, *ma chérie*. In fact, it was more than acceptable." He reached over to her, and she closed her eyes, expecting him to caress her face. But when the feeling of his hand didn't reach her, she opened them again and blinked in confusion. A cynical smile played over his face, and his fingers clutched a sizeable green leaf which he waved in her face. "You would not wish to return to the ballroom with this in your coiffure, mademoiselle. People would talk."

He flicked the offending leaf away and, again, Eugenie blushed.

She felt compelled to explain her behavior.

"I was merely making certain you were not engaging in an assignation, that's all."

"And why would that be of interest to you, mademoiselle?" De Lacey's eyes gleamed in amusement and Eugenie realized she had given away more than she intended.

"No reason," she replied with an air.

"If I kiss you again will you tell me the reason?"

She felt the color suffuse her face again. Wanting to reply both yes and no, she posed a question instead.

"Why was that man threatening you, vicomte?"

At this, de Lacey's face darkened. "He wasn't."

"No, you're right. He was just delivering a message."

De Lacey glared at her. "Just what did you hear,

mademoiselle?" His dark eyes bored into hers and his mouth, just a moment ago so soft and yielding, settled into a hard line. Eugenie grew a little afraid.

"Nothing I could understand."

"What did you hear?" De Lacey took her arms and shook her just a little, his voice quieter, sharper. Her eyes opened wide in fear.

"Please, monsieur, let me go, I heard nothing. Just a request for you to go somewhere, and you say you would not."

After a long moment, de Lacey let her go. "My apologies, mademoiselle. I should not have frightened you so."

"I was not afraid." However, there was a quiver in her voice that she chose to disregard. "I should return to the ballroom now."

"Indeed." De Lacey smiled, and his lips once again tempted Eugenie. She felt no desire at all to return to the ballroom. In fact, there was only one desire she wished to accede to, a shocking, debauched desire, but one that she had no power over.

"Will you kiss me again, monsieur?" she asked, both coy and shy at once.

De Lacey required no other invitation. Again, she found herself enveloped in his powerful arms, breathing in his scent— something oriental, spiced and maybe a hint of musk. It was intoxicating, as were his lips bearing down on hers.

His kisses burned through her to the very end of her nerves. They curled into her brain like thick gray smoke, blotting out all reason. The one focal point, where their lips met, was the only thing she could hear or see or feel. His lips, his taste with its echoes of brandy, fell around her in a heady fog. She was trapped, captured by his caress. And she never wanted to be free.

He, too, seemed to have difficulty disentangling himself from Eugenie's embrace. His harsh breathing and the deep sharp fire in his eyes showed that he, too, was affected by the kiss. Yet he pulled away, setting Eugenie a little away from him, and running one hand through his hair.

"You should most assuredly return to the ballroom now,

mademoiselle, before all of my control disintegrates."

"Would that be so disastrous?" She wanted more of this intoxicating experience, but to her disappointment, de Lacey shook his head. "It would be cataclysmic, Eugenie." He picked up and played with one of her golden curls, before dropping it, and reiterating, "Back to the ballroom with you. I'll be along shortly."

He then disappeared into the dark greenery, and Eugenie was left to find her way back to the ballroom, thoroughly warmed, and thoroughly confused.

CHAPTER THIRTEEN

De Lacey chuckled as he watched Eugenie run back to the ballroom. The innocent wench. He could tell she was inexperienced, in fact, he would lay money down that he had been her very first kiss. Still, she showed spirit, and he liked that. He would need a wife who could offer him some enjoyment outside the bedroom. Eugenie continued to rise in his estimation.

Despite the innocence of her kiss, de Lacey had noted her passion, the way her young body had responded to the new feelings pulsing through it. It would be fascinating to school her in the art of lovemaking.

De Lacey was still chuckling when he arrived home several hours later. Eugenie had made a point to avoid him for the rest of the evening, even going so far as to refuse the dance they had organized, insisting she had never agreed to such a thing. Instead, he danced with her friend, Lady Felicity, who despite her middling looks, was a lovely person and only too happy to talk about Eugenie.

Tatillion met him at the door. "Good evening, monsieur. Did you have an enjoyable evening?" He helped de Lacey out of his coat and took his hat.

"Tatillion, I had a wonderful evening." The smile wouldn't leave his face, and another laugh bubbled up to the surface.

Tatillion's eye's narrowed. "Mademoiselle Ponnette?"

"Of course."

"What did you do?"

"My dear fellow, I did nothing. Mademoiselle followed me. It was she who misbehaved."

Tatillion shook his head. "I fear where this is going."

"She thought I was engaging in a tryst. I wasn't. And I taught her a lesson about young ladies following gentlemen out into the garden."

Tatillion groaned. "Did you frighten her off?"

De Lacey snorted. "Frighten? Her? The lady has more gumption than ten men. She was a little stunned by the turn of events, but not frightened in the least."

"Hmm." Tatillion seemed unconvinced. He poured de Lacey a glass of brandy.

"She will make the perfect wife, just as soon as I rid myself of these bothersome smugglers."

"Bothersome smugglers? You mean the ones who beat you to a pulp and broke your wrist?"

"You always make things sound worse than they are, Tatillion. I mean the ones who thought they were teaching me a lesson, but who instead, hardened my resolve to exit their company. All I need to do now is come up with a plan as to how to do that."

Tatillion prowled around the room, turning a lamp up here, lighting a taper there, fixing and tidying as he went. "You could just disappear. Not attend when they call."

De Lacey considered for a moment. "No, that wouldn't work. I'm too well known in London." He frowned into his brandy. "It needs to be something that will disrupt their business, so that I have the upper hand, even if just for a moment."

The two men were silent as they contemplated the problem.

"I have it!" said de Lacey. "We interrupt their supply into London."

Tatillion looked skeptical. "And how exactly do we do that? And who exactly is this 'we' you speak of?"

"Tatillion, show some enthusiasm, for goodness sake. We hold up the coaches they send via the London Road and dispose of the goods. That way, their supply will be disrupted, and their customers will get annoyed with them."

"And they, in turn, will get annoyed with us. Very annoyed."

"Ah, but they won't know who we are because we will be dressed as highwaymen."

"Highwaymen?" Tatillion spat out the word as if it tasted terrible. "You expect me to dress as a highwayman?"

De Lacey could almost see the fashionista in Tatillion rebelling. "Yes, because I order you to do so. It's a brilliant idea, Tatillion. We go in, steal or smash the valuables and ride away before they can do anything about it. You can exercise your considerable Savate skills on the arms and legs of the outriders, and I can exercise mine on the drivers."

"Still, it sounds tricky. How will you remain undiscovered?"

"Masks, my good friend. We will wear handkerchiefs across our faces."

"And how will they know it was you damaging their supply runs if we are disguised?"

"When enough damage has been done, I will reveal myself and advise them that I will stop just as soon as they release me from all contact with the gang."

Tatillion shook his head slowly. "I don't like it, monsieur. It sounds like considerable danger for maybe less than satisfactory return. And the clothes." He shuddered. "The clothes I will have to wear."

"Your finicky dress sense will have to take a side seat to your love for your master for a while, Tatillion," said de Lacey. He hadn't felt this alive in months. With the kisses of a pretty girl on his lips and the prospect of adventure, he couldn't wait for the morning so he could set his plan in place.

Tatillion tsked and replied, "You are lucky, monsieur, that my love for you extends to such things. Filthy cravats, tricorns and," he shuddered, "handkerchiefs across our faces. It's enough to make a grown manservant weep in despair."

CHAPTER FOURTEEN

"Stand and deliver!"

The shot of a revolver rang out, and even through his kerchief, de Lacey could smell the tang of gunpowder.

The horse leading the laden cart whinnied in fear at the noise and shied, the driver only just holding the cart upright as the horse skittered sideways across the road.

The man beside the driver reached for his gun, but a click by his temple made him pause. A soft voice said, "I do not think that would be wise, sir."

De Lacey kept his gun trained on the driver, who looked at him with abject hatred. "Highwaymen. You are scum." He spat over the side of the cart.

De Lacey merely replied in a strident tone, trying to keep as much of his accent from his voice as possible, "Unload the goods and roll them into the bushes at the side of the road."

"You've got to be raggin' me. I ain't unloadin' the goods."

"Fine." De Lacey took aim, and the men jumped as one of the barrels behind them trickled deep, red wine from the hole de Lacey fired in it. "If you do not do what I tell you, the next bullet hole will be in your belly."

Grumbling, the two men got down and relieved the cart of its cargo—twelve barrels in all, as well as several rolls of fine silks. Tatillion took a moment to remove any weapons that were ensconced within.

"You are foolish gentlemen to be messin' with the Waldershare

Gang," sneered one of the louts.

"Waldershare Gang? Isn't that one of the little smuggling rackets out of Kent?" De Lacey feigned ignorance.

"Little smuggling ring? My friend, if they work out who you are—and they will—they have a hundred men at the ready to track you down."

De Lacey replied with a dainty yawn, the back of his hand against his mouth. "As you can see, I am terrified of your little gang. Now, since you are done, Umberto?" He addressed Tatillion. "Can you see to it that their horse is relieved of its traces?" Tatillion nodded and reached for the reins.

Just at that moment, one of the men made a run directly at Tatillion's horse, pulling him off and dragging him to the ground. The horse reared up on its hind legs and ran off.

De Lacey's hand wavered, but he kept the pistol trained on the other man. He knew Tatillion was a skilled fighter, but he also knew there was a gun in the middle of the scuffle between the two men. If the lout got hold of it, Tatillion might well be saying good day to his maker well before his allotted time.

The two men were on their feet now, circling each other, the fight more menacing for the silence between the two men. Both wore snarling grimaces, and the other man sported a long red mark high on his cheekbone—evidence that Tatillion had managed to hit him before they got up.

The man reached out with a punch, which Tatillion evaded before the man's other fist came at him, catching him a glancing blow on the chin. De Lacey gasped, but Tatillion managed to stagger back and regain his stance.

The other man smiled, obviously feeling as if he was winning. He stopped fighting, and spat on each of his hands in turn, rubbing them together, then snarled, "Come on then you robber filth. Bring it on."

Tatillion seemed to sense an advantage and closed on the other man. While slight, Tatillion was muscular, and trained in the Savate style, using both arms and legs, hands and feet in an attempt to disable his opponent.

To de Lacey, the fight seemed to last for hours, but it was over in moments. Tatillion swept one leg around, and connected with the other man's kneecap, which cracked with a loud 'pop!' The man fell to the ground, swearing in agony and rage. Tatillion strode over to him and punched him hard in the face—twice.

De Lacey very nearly cheered, then recalled his position. Having been so caught up in watching the fight, he had forgotten to keep his eye on their other prisoner. Luckily for de Lacey, the other man had also been entranced by the spectacle.

He waved toward the man on the ground. "Take your friend and get out of here, before we do much worse."

The man lifted his friend from the ground and, bearing most of his weight, hobbled away, cursing de Lacey and Tatillion. "You won't get away with this. Only the most foolish of highwaymen would dare to mess with the Waldershare Gang. Your time is limited."

Indifferent to their threats, de Lacey fired a shot just over their heads, which sent the two men hobbling away at a quicker pace.

De Lacey and Tatillion watched until they were gone, and then turned to each other.

Tatillion pulled the kerchief from his mouth and spat in disgust. "Pah! How does one continue to breathe inside that disgusting thing? And to fight? I thought I was going to die from lack of air."

De Lacey laughed, and grabbed his arm, shaking his hand hard. "We did it, Tatillion! We held up a cart!"

"Well of course we did, monsieur," replied Tatillion, frowning at de Lacey. "What did you expect? That we would dance a cotillion?"

"What are we going to do with the barrels? And the silks?"

Tatillion tapped a finger to the side of his nose. "Leave those to me, monsieur. I know exactly what to do with them. Now, you should make your way to The Ancient Crow."

"There's plenty of time. They have a good two or three hours of walking ahead of them."

"Perhaps, but you must be at the taven well before they get there."

"What would I do without you, Tatillion?"

"I suspect you would fail in every endeavor you attempted," replied Tatillion. De Lacey laughed and slapped his back, at which action Tatillion looked offended. He raised one supercilious eyebrow, which caused de Lacey to laugh all the more.

"I do believe you're right, my old friend."

CHAPTER FIFTEEN

The tankards were raised as usual at The Ancient Crow that night, but de Lacey could feel the undercurrents of discontent beneath the merrymaking. The two men from the cart had hobbled their way back to Ashford, where de Lacey had already arrived hours before, changed out of his highwayman garb, and been as shocked as the rest at their untimely interruption of the festivities.

De Lacey was pleased to see that the men didn't seem to recognize him as one of the bandits. He silently thanked Tatillion again—the costumes were perfect. The kerchiefs across their mouths had muffled their voices, and by the time he was fully dressed, the only thing one would notice of Jean de Lacey was his eyes, which peered out from under a dark tricorne.

Cheers died away, and the talk moved to worried murmurs.

De Lacey approached Arthur and the ringleaders at their table.

"Draw and quarter them," growled one man.

"You'd have to track 'em down first."

"Maybe this is a one off."

"Maybe they didn't know it was contraband." One man was prepared to give the thieves the benefit of the doubt.

"They would've known soon as they looked in the back of the cart."

"It doesn't make sense for thieves to steal from us."

"No, it doesn't." Arthur's voice rang out strongly amongst the worried men. "But it was a modest load, so we'll make some inquiries, make sure it wasn't another gang, but we shall continue as if it never happened."

The other men, whether thoughtful or worried at Arthur's pronouncement, nodded their assent. As their leader, his words were law. It worked well that way. There had to be one man right at the top, and Arthur had fought hard to get there. Three former leaders lay in their graves—at Arthur's hand it was said—so that he could ascend to the top. No one was prepared to naysay his words.

"Cheers to that," said de Lacey, pulling up a stool at the table and lifting his tankard. The others started at his injection into the conversation and then allowed themselves to toast.

Arthur stared at him under drawn shaggy brows, then slowly lifted his own tankard. De Lacey stared back at him, realizing that this was the first time they had seen him since the beating.

He wondered what was going through Arthur's sharp mind behind the brows. Did he suspect de Lacey? Had he put two and two together? De Lacey's face didn't change, but concern welled in his chest.

"Are you back then, Frenchie?" Arthur asked softly.

"Aye," replied de Lacey, imitating the affirmative used by the rough men.

"For good?"

"Aye."

There was a long silence.

"Good." Arthur raised his tankard toward de Lacey "To the French!"

"To the French!" The toast roared out across the tavern.

Before de Lacey could reply, there was a shout. "Bugger the French." To his surprise, Maggie came striding up to him, as the men stepped out of her way. She had a look of fury on her face such as he had never seen before. In her hands, were several news sheets, and she threw them down on the table in front of de Lacey, then stood glaring at him, hands on hips.

"Well?" she demanded.

"You're in for it now, lad," one of the men at the table

murmured, and the others agreed.

De Lacey looked at the papers. They were the usual London social rags—silly things that reported the goings on of the upper classes: engagements, weddings, balls, gossip.

Gossip. De Lacey picked up the top paper.

'The Vicomte Landreville found himself in a predicament of late when at Lord Grantby's ball, he all but fainted in front of several ladies. However, it seems the device worked in his favor, for he was later seen being coddled by Mademoiselle Ponnette, recent *émigré* and the daughter of Baron Ponnette. The mademoiselle was most solicitous, and it would seem from their close association that a declaration should be expected at any moment.'

The other articles were the same. Discussions about how many dances he and Eugenie had shared, the balls they had attended together, and there was even some mention of the wagers at Brooks's.

De Lacey looked up at Maggie who was still fuming. "What, Maggie? I don't understand."

"You don't under—? Why are you chasing this French whore all over town?"

His voice hardened. "You will never speak of Mademoiselle Ponnette in such a way."

"I'll speak of her how ever I want. Do I mean nothing to you?"

De Lacey frowned in confusion. "I still don't understand. Why are you so upset?"

"Don't you care that I'm the laughingstock of Ashford?"

It was true, several of the men were guffawing into their tankards. De Lacey stood.

"Come, *chérie*, we should discuss this elsewhere." While he wasn't ashamed of his actions, he didn't need his love affairs aired in front of these fellows. It was unmanly.

Both he and Maggie stomped over to a spot behind the counter, out of the way of the patrons.

"Now, what's this all about, Maggie? You knew I was planning to marry."

"Yes, but you were going to marry me."

"I never was. I told you. You know it."

"But you…" She blushed. "You lay with me."

He raised one eyebrow. "I hardly think I was the first, *chérie,*" he replied dryly. "Ask one of your other swains to marry you."

Her face drained of color. "How dare you say such a thing to me?"

His voice hardened. "Because it's the truth, mademoiselle. You were hardly an untried partner."

"But you said you loved me."

"I did no such thing." De Lacey quickly thought back over their liaisons, seeking to assure himself that, even in the throes of passion, he had not said such a thing.

"You did too. When you came in here all beaten and bruised. I cared for you then, I bound your wounds and comforted you. And you said you loved me."

De Lacey flicked his hand in the air. "I remember little from that entire evening, Maggie. If in fact I did say it, and I'm not saying that I did, you cannot hold me to it. I was delirious with pain."

"I will hold you to it," she declared. "You love me. And I love you."

De Lacey was starting to feel impatient. "I do not love you, and I am not about to throw my heritage away on an English farm girl. I've told you that before."

"I'll tell her," Maggie said, a strange brightness in her eyes. "I'll go to London and find her, and tell her that you slept with me— frequently. And that you love me, and not her. That you're planning to marry me, not her."

De Lacey allowed his indifference to seep in his voice. "Do as you wish, Maggie. I cannot stop you." Of course, he could never allow her to do it. Eugenie might believe her, which would cause all kinds of complications. But he had to make her understand that she meant nothing to him.

"I'll do it," she continued, "You see if I don't."

"Fine, then, you do it." De Lacey went to walk away, but she gripped his arm.

"You're mine, Jean de Lacey," she said fiercely. He regarded her with a cold, haughty look and shook her hand off his arm, before turning away and rejoining his table of friends.

"Women," he said, as he sat down and shrugged.

The other men murmured their agreement.

CHAPTER SIXTEEN

Eugenie tapped her tiny foot impatiently. It had been three days since she had seen the vicomte, three days of wondering where he was, what he was doing and whether he was ever going to kiss her again. Three days of garden parties, dinners, entertainments, and of course, endless balls. Like this one. Eugenie couldn't even remember whose ball she was attending, there had been so many of them. All exactly the same, and all terribly boring without the amusement of the company of Vicomte Landreville.

As De Lacey walked into the ballroom alongside Lord Edenburgh, she frowned even deeper. He seemed to have a glow about him as if he had been refreshed somehow. She was even more intrigued and more than a little piqued. How dare Vicomte Landreville look as if he had been enjoying himself? It was just like a gentleman to go off and have a good time without the company of his...

His what? Eugenie chided herself. It was not as if he had declared himself.

He caught her eye and smiled across the room, and all of Eugenie's doubts dissolved in a second. She was vaguely aware that Lord Edenburgh noticed the exchange as well, and a little secret smile crossed his face, but she was far too pleased by the vicomte's attention to be embarrassed. After all, a lady should be happy to be singled out by the gentleman she favored.

It took all of her willpower to keep from hurtling herself across the ballroom to pepper him with questions, but she managed it.

Surely the vicomte wouldn't keep her waiting long.

Thankfully, after greeting their host, the vicomte and Lord Edenburgh made their way through the crowd to where Eugenie and Felicity were standing beside Aunt Lucinda.

As was proper, the vicomte allowed Lord Edenburgh to greet them first.

"My dear Lady Felicity, Mademoiselle Ponnette. How do you do this evening?" The earl bowed over each of their hands in turn, bestowing his usual friendly smile on them. "I do hope both of you ladies will save me a dance this evening?"

While Felicity murmured her usual acquiescence, Eugenie smiled widely at him. "Of course, my lord. However, I am afraid you might have to organized around Monsieur Landreville."

At hearing her words, de Lacey's face lit up. He was in the middle of a quiet how-do-you-do to Felicity, but he straightened and turned to Eugenie with a smile.

"Mademoiselle, you honor me. Now, let me see." He tapped his lip with his finger. "Which dance would Lord Edenburgh particularly want to dance with you? I shall choose that one, and the first, if that doesn't inconvenience you?"

"That's not very nice, monsieur," she chided, amused. "After all, Lord Edenburgh is an earl, and you are merely a vicomte. Should you not give way to his greater claims?"

"His greater claims? I should think not. I fear my claims on you are significantly greater than his."

Eugenie blushed. The vicomte's words were very close to a declaration.

"Indeed, monsieur? How do you conclude thus?" Lord Edenburgh turned on de Lacey with one amused, raised eyebrow. The vicomte seemed to realize that his teasing had taken a turn toward the serious, for he flushed, then laughed. "My apologies, I do believe I have tripped over my own tongue."

Eugenie nodded. "*Oui*, monsieur, that you have. It is surprising that I am not prostrate on the floor from shock at your words."

"Thankfully, mademoiselle, you do not appear to me to be a lady much affected by shock."

"It is true," she replied mournfully. "I am far too sensible for artfulness. It would never cross my mind to fall at your feet, or even to pretend to faint into your arms."

"Pity," murmured de Lacey, taking her hand and bowing. He brushed his lips over it, keeping her eyes locked in a wicked gaze. Eugenie felt herself smiling and blushing furiously. This was the most animated she had ever seen de Lacey—the most publicly flirtatious he had ever been as well. She hoped that meant he had come to some conclusion of his own accord, and that he would offer shortly.

The orchestra completed their warm-up and started to play, and de Lacey offered his arm to Eugenie. "Shall we?" He said. She was pleased to see Felicity taking Lord Edenburgh's arm as well, even though it would probably be one of the few dances she would have. Poor Felicity. Once Eugenie's own happiness was assured, she would have to turn her attention to finding that elusive gentleman who would look beyond Felicity's outward appearance.

She happily danced in de Lacey's arms, oblivious to the rest of the dancers. She felt carefree and scandalously happy. However, her thoughts were clouded by a question that crossed her mind.

"Monsieur, where have you been these past days? I looked for you at three different events, and you were at none."

He grinned, the wicked look returning to his eyes. "I was off with my lover, of course."

She feigned shock. "You should not sully the ears of innocents with such talk."

"My apologies. I was off tending to my sheep. I have quite a large flock of them in a pen at Hertfordshire."

"Really?"

"No."

She sighed. "You really are the most irritating of men."

"Ah, but that is what makes me interesting and mysterious, mademoiselle. Imagine if there were no secret to me? I should be tedious and proper."

"Yes, but at least I wouldn't stay awake at night wondering

where you were."

"I keep you awake at night? How interesting."

Eugenie realized again that she had let herself say more than she should. She blushed and frowned at de Lacey. "It would be significantly more gentlemanly if you didn't notice when I said things I ought not."

"But much less amusing, *ma chérie*."

"When are you going to tell me where you go? It's driving me mad."

She turned all her wiles on him, opening her large blue eyes wide and pouting prettily, and de Lacey moaned.

"How am I supposed to keep my secrets when you make yourself so delectable?" he said.

"So, you'll tell me?"

He smiled at her eagerness. "No. I will not tell you."

She trod on his foot, then gave him a wide smile when he grunted in pain. "*Excusez-moi*, monsieur. I seem to have forgotten the steps again for a moment."

"As I have forgotten your penchant for violence when you don't get your own way." His smile was slightly pained. "I do adore dancing with you, mademoiselle. It is so very challenging."

"And will continue to be, so long as you refuse to tell me what you do when you are away."

"I shall ensure my feet are prepared for the onslaught."

After securing the supper dance, Eugenie watched as de Lacey made his bow and wandered away with Lord Edenburgh. Felicity sighed beside her, and Eugenie turned, only to see her friend also studying the two gentlemen.

"*Mon amie*, what is it?" she asked, tucking her arm into Felicity's.

Felicity frowned. "I don't know. Quincey seemed distracted today. And when I asked him what it was, he just smiled and said there was a problem with his brandy delivery. Of all things."

Eugenie's eyebrows lifted. "That's very odd, for a gentleman like Lord Edenburgh. He is usually the very epitome of decorum."

"Yes. I look forward to our dance. It's usually the only chance I have for normal conversation across the whole evening." Felicity's tone was self-deprecating, and Eugenie took her arm and squeezed.

"My dear, I'm sure that's not true. You always secure a few dances. Well, sometimes, anyway."

"Yes, and they make either very old and boring or very ugly and stupid partners." Felicity's dislike of the situation was written across her face.

"Really? Does one go with the other?"

"What do you mean?"

"So, are all old gentlemen boring, and all ugly men stupid?"

Felicity managed to produce a wan smile. "Sometimes they are all of those at once."

Eugenie shuddered. "Heavens."

Felicity straightened her shoulders. "Now, tell me about your vicomte."

Eugenie flushed. "He's not my vicomte."

Felicity snorted. "Of course he is. Maybe not officially, but there is no doubt. Did you find out where he has been?"

Eugenie sought the vicomte out from the crowd, and when she located him, she narrowed her eyes at him. "No, I have not, and it's driving me to distraction."

At just that moment, Lady Hampshire joined them, waving her fan with some speed.

"My lady, are you alright?" Eugenie asked.

The lady smiled wickedly. "Yes, I'm fine, only I felt terribly faint, so I had to deny Lord Turnbull the remainder of our dance and come over to sit it out with my kindest of friends."

Eugenie smiled. "I understand. Shall we sit?" She motioned to a chaise a few steps away, and the three ladies deposited themselves.

"Thank you, my dears. Lord Turnbull was starting to resemble an octopus."

Felicity frowned, returning to the previous topic of conversation. "It really is a puzzle. Why on earth would he not tell you, unless he was engaged in something nefarious?"

"That is the point exactly," replied Eugenie with warmth.

"Who are we talking about?" inquired Lady Hampshire.

Before Eugenie could motion her to silence, Felicity replied, "Vicomte Landreville. He keeps disappearing and refuses to tell Eugenie where he has been."

"Which of course there is no requirement for him to do since there is nothing between us," Eugenie added desperately.

Lady Hampshire's tinkling laugh brought the color to Eugenie's cheek even as she smiled in response.

"My dear, where would we be if we had no secrets? What a boring life we would all lead!" Lady Hampshire confided behind her fan, "Why I don't suppose I told more than a third of my secrets to my husband, and he was as dear to me as any man could have been."

"Then it's acceptable for a man to have secrets from his wife?" Eugenie asked.

"Of course. If he did not, what possible reason could we give for keeping our own secrets?"

There was no chance for further discussion, as first one gentleman then another came to make their bow to the ladies, and to ask Lady Hampshire and Eugenie for the next dance.

Eugenie noticed the next two young ladies that the vicomte danced with—wispy, brainless debutantes who simpered and giggled under his gaze. She smiled to herself to see the boredom descend over his face and the sharp elbow and words that he had for Lord Edenburgh each time the dance finished. It seemed Lord Edenburgh was enjoying fobbing the vicomte off to the irritating girls while he took advantage of the lovelier ones.

While Eugenie certainly enjoyed her dances and had to pay some scant attention to her partners, at no time was she unaware of the vicomte's place in the room. So, it was no surprise that she noticed when he and Lord Edenburgh slowly made their way to a door that led to the upstairs stairwell. She assumed he and the earl would escape up there perhaps for a brandy. She didn't truly know what gentleman did in the upper rooms, having never been there herself during a ball.

"I'm forming a terrible idea in my head," she whispered to Felicity, who groaned.

"Oh no. What is it?"

"The vicomte is about to go upstairs. I'm going to creep up behind and listen in on his conversation."

Felicity looked shocked. "You can't do that. What if someone sees you? Your reputation will be in tatters."

Eugenie regarded Felicity with pity. "*Mon amie*, do you not see how it could be perfect? I might get the information I need to set my mind at ease. If anyone sees me, there is no impropriety, since there will be two gentlemen in the room. I fail to see the issue. And I must know if he has a lover, Felicity. It is so important to my future happiness."

Felicity shook her head. "I don't suppose anything I say is going to change your mind, is it?"

"No, I am afraid not," Eugenie's tone was a little mournful, but her eyes sparkled. "You could accompany me."

"Absolutely not. Not only would I be terrified, but I'm sure my gangly limbs would knock something over or give us away somehow. No, if you insist on playing spy, you should do it alone. I'll be waiting right over there, with the other wallflowers." She started to walk away, fanning her face.

Eugenie smiled at her retreating friend before skirting the ballroom, trying to stay hidden in doorways behind floral arrangements, and in small enclosures. In a tucked away corner, she surprised a young couple in a passionate embrace.

"Imagine that I'm not even here," she said in a sepulchral tone to the embarrassed lovers, before skittering away to another hiding place.

Here she paused. She could see the backs of Lord Edenburgh and Monsieur Landreville. It seemed they had been detained by some of their acquaintances. She would have to shuffle past them to get to the stairwell.

Eugenie took a deep breath and before she could think about it further, launched herself toward them, murmuring an, 'Excuse me," as she flitted past and into the quiet of the stairwell. She realized her heart was beating quite erratically and laughed gently to herself. It had been a while since she'd had an adventure, and she was enjoying it. In Paris, as a young woman of virtue, the only way to have any fun at all had been to escape the confines of her station, which she had done as often as she had dared. Eugenie had visited bazaars, fairs and masked balls that nobody had suspected her of attending. However, she had never before had an adventure involving a gentleman. That was a new experience.

Eugenie trotted up the stairs, knowing that here she was quite exposed. Once she reached the upper corridor, she could relax more, and when she found a hiding place in the intended room, she could settle down altogether.

The room at the end of the hall looked like a library and was the only one with open doors. Eugenie swiftly ensconced herself behind the heavy azure curtains in the window, and a little squeak escaped her as a small spider skittered across her arm. Eugenie shuddered. She was not afraid of tiny spiders, but she wasn't too fond of them touching her. She reflected that in her own house, she would be sure her maids were cleaning properly—especially just before a ball.

Eugenie heard the approach of masculine voices, and stood very still, hoping that her thumping heart wouldn't be heard by the gentlemen.

"Good God, these routs will be the death of me." Lord Edenburgh lowered himself into the comfortable settee, as de Lacey poured them both a drink from the crystal decanter at the side of the room.

Handing him the drink, de Lacey breathed in deeply. "Can you smell a little something feminine in here?" The earl laughed as de Lacey raised one eyebrow.

"Do you suppose we interrupted a tryst?"

"No, it must have been well over by the time we arrived. I didn't see anyone in the hallway." With a sigh, de Lacey sat in a nearby chair, taking a sip from his own drink.

"Ah, quality French brandy. I always knew Granville had good taste."

"And you know how he procures it, don't you?" At de Lacey's head shake the earl leaned forward and continued sotto voice. "He has a supplier who smuggles it in."

"Really," drawled de Lacey.

"Yes. I've even heard that the smugglers use Granville's outbuildings as a store while they are distributing."

"Is that so?" De Lacey kept his tone light.

Lord Edenburgh leaned back and groaned. "How many balls and parties do you think we've been to this season?" The long-suffering tone of his voice made de Lacey laugh out loud.

"Far too many, my friend. However, there is the upside of being able to lay a finger on the ladies you are interested in and hold more than a formal conversation. If it weren't for balls and parties, we would be completely cut off from all feminine touch."

"Speak for yourself," said the earl comfortably. "I have the lovely Miss Leerie waiting for me over in her rooms on Norfolk Square."

"You mean your actress friend?"

"Of course. Who else would I mean?"

De Lacey shrugged. "Yes, but you have the money to set up with a mistress, my friend. I do not." What he didn't confess was that he had no desire to find a mistress either.

"What about your Mademoiselle Ponnette? She seems to be smitten with you? Couldn't you beguile her into joining you in the gardens for a moment or two? I had heard your prowess with the ladies was second to none, my friend. Have you lost your touch?" It was all said in jest. However, de Lacey felt hot under the collar for a moment, and his friend's face a suitable punching bag. He swallowed down the inclination.

De Lacey produced a tight smile, but his attention was caught by a very slight movement in the darkened corner of the room. He peered into the gloom, trying to see what had moved. The night, however, refused to give up her secrets, and de Lacey wasn't interested in getting up from his comfortable chair to investigate further, so he put it from his mind.

"Mademoiselle Ponnette is above my touch, Quincey. She's far too proper to engage in such a thing."

"May the good Lord save us from the proper little miss," replied the earl with a theatrical shiver, which set de Lacey's teeth on edge. He turned the conversation back around.

"Tell me more about Granville's nefarious behavior."

The earl shrugged. "There's little more to tell. I believe his suppliers come in somewhere on the Kent coast. They bring the barrels in two at a time strapped across the chests of a hundred men. They transport them to London, and the gang has a distribution network from there. It's all done in one night, and Granville receives a barrel or two of fine brandy for the trouble." He held up his glass and regarded the dark liquid in the firelight. "Everyone does it, de Lacey. If they don't get it direct from the gangs, they get it further down the supply chain. Even old Reverend Nightingale has been known to be the recipient of a drop or two from time to time."

"And you?"

"Of course. Although I buy mine from a reputable merchant."

"Reputable?"

The earl chuckled at de Lacey's incredulous expression. "Well, as reputable as can be expected."

De Lacey shook his head. "So, this smuggling is beneficial?"

Lord Edenburgh frowned. "I'm not sure I would like to comment on the ethics of the thing, old man. Certainly, we hear from the pulpit that stealing will send us straight to hell. But is it stealing when one is merely avoiding the efforts of government to fund their armies? Or is it civil disobedience?" He took a sip of his brandy. "Either way, my conscience is clear. I buy from a reputable source. My hands are clean."

Studying the contents of his own glass, de Lacey frowned. "I wish I could say the same," he muttered.

"I beg your pardon? What was that?"

"Nothing."

He felt little better than a common thief with his involvement in the smuggling ring. Back in France, he had always been a law-abiding citizen, a lawyer, in fact. And he felt a little guilty for reducing the income of a government who had welcomed him in when his own country had made it clear he was very much unwelcome. It was a quandary, certainly.

"Well," said the earl, downing the last of the liquor in his glass, "I suppose we had better find our way back to the ballroom. The matchmakers will have noticed we are missing by now."

"You go," said de Lacey. "I'll be down shortly."

"Don't be too long. You don't want to keep Mademoiselle Ponnette waiting."

De Lacey snorted. "Mademoiselle Ponnette has far and away enough admirers to not even notice if I am there."

There was a gleam in the earl's eye. "Do you want to bet on it?"

De Lacey put his glass down and his hands up in front of him. "No, Quincey, I do not want to bet on it."

"Why not, old boy? No confidence in your own prowess?"

De Lacey glared at Lord Edenburgh as he continued, a wicked smile on his face. "I'm going to enter into the betting book at Brooks's tomorrow that I believe you will be married to Miss Ponnette within three months."

This time, de Lacey was sure he heard a gasp from the dark corner. His head snapped around, but again, the darkness stymied his efforts.

"I would prefer that you didn't, my friend," he said seriously, his gaze returning to the earl. However, his friend merely snapped his fingers and, with a laugh, exited the room.

CHAPTER SEVENTEEN

As soon as the earl was gone, de Lacey stood and prowled the dark edges of the room. Perhaps the couple whose tryst they may have interrupted were in fact still there, waiting for them to leave so they could continue their liaison. He certainly didn't begrudge them that, but his curiosity was piqued as to who it might be hiding in the shadows.

There! He saw the whiteness of a lady's arm jerk back behind the heavy curtain. He moved silently forward, holding his breath, the thrill of the hunt upon him. His eyes were fixed on his prey. With a flourish, he pulled back the curtain. The laughter in his eyes died, and an oath of disapproval passed his lips.

"*Mon dieu*, mademoiselle. What on earth are you doing hiding up here? Do you not know how your reputation might suffer?" His eyes narrowed. "Who are you here with?"

"There is no one else here, monsieur, I assure you." Eugenie stepped out from her window hiding place, head held high. She had never looked so lovely, with her hair a little disheveled by the curtain, and her color high. De Lacey found it difficult not to take her in his arms. Instead, he crossed his arms over his chest and stared at Eugenie disapprovingly.

"Were you spying on me again, mademoiselle?"

"No, I was not. Don't be so conceited." The lady moved as if to make her way to the door, but de Lacey blocked her progress.

"Well, if you were not spying on me, then whom? Or was there to be a meeting, only the gentleman didn't appear?"

98

De Lacey wasn't sure whether he wanted to hear the result of his query.

"Even if there was supposed to be, you and Lord Edenburgh put paid to that, didn't you?" Mademoiselle Ponnette seemed ruffled. De Lacey kept his arms firmly crossed over himself. He wished nothing more than to take her in his arms and smooth her feathers. But he knew if he did so, he might not be able to stop himself from taking more liberties than the lady wished. Then again, the lady was certainly putting herself in a position where she might expect such treatment. His anger burned. What was she doing here? How could she have so little regard for her own good name?

"So, there was an assignation?" He heard the harsh tone in his voice. Good. The silly little *ingenue* needed to hear it.

He heard Eugenie sigh. "No. There wasn't. I just... I needed to get away from the ballroom for a moment." She cast her eyes down and then looked back up at de Lacey from under them.

"I quite understand, mademoiselle. The noise and heat from the ballroom are what brought Lord Edenburgh and myself up here as well. A short break from them can often provide one with the stamina to continue for the rest of the night. But not for young ladies of good breeding." While his words were smooth, he narrowed his eyes at her, still battling his anger at her lack of propriety.

He smoothly walked to the door and closed it.

Eugenie's eye's boggled. "What are you doing?" She sounded scandalized.

He stood in front of her, allowing his anger to blaze. "What on earth were you thinking, Eugenie? Do you know what would happen if you were discovered up here? Your reputation would be ruined."

"And that is why I was hiding behind the curtain, monsieur." Her eyes threw sparks at him, and he was reminded of a ferocious little pea hen he used to own that would attack, pecking anyone in her way until they bled. "And what do you mean by closing the door?"

"Merely ensuring that we are not discovered in a compromise, mademoiselle. With the door open, anyone passing by could find us ensconced cozily together. With it closed, at least you have time to regain your hiding place, should the door handle be shaken."

Eugenie seemed to consider and agree with his reasoning.

"In that case, we might as well be comfortable." She stepped away from the window and walked to one of the leather settees, settling herself down on it and, removing her shoes, tucking her feet up under her. De Lacey, disarmed by her innocence and lack of pretense, felt his anger melt away. She would be a lovely little wife, and if her passion in the garden was any indication, a wonderful bed partner as well.

His thoughts were interrupted by the object of his internal discourse.

"Would you be able to bring me a small glass of that brandy, monsieur?"

Her voice sounded combative as if she expected de Lacey to refuse. He suspected she had never touched brandy before, and rather than wishing to shield her from her first taste of the beverage, he moved with alacrity to pour her a small measure.

She took the glass from him dubiously. "Is that all I get?" she asked. She swirled the contents of the glass.

De Lacey laughed. "Maybe you should try that before you say anything."

Eugenie put the glass to her lips and tipped a good portion of the liquid into her mouth. Before she could even swallow, her eyes rounded and she spat the spirit back into the glass. "It burns!" she gasped.

"Yes," said de Lacey, taking a long swallow of his own. "It does. That's the charm of it."

"There is no charm in that," replied Eugenie, her eyes watering. "How can something that burns be charming?"

"I know of many charming things that can burn." De Lacey looked at her over the edge of his glass, his eyebrow raised. She flushed, understanding the subtle nuances of his words, but feigning innocence.

"Indeed, I have no idea of what you speak, monsieur."

"Really?"

"Yes really."

"You interest me, mademoiselle."

"Oh?" Eugenie's eyes sparkled. De Lacey had to smile at her instant enthusiasm.

"Yes. You pretend that you are all that is pure and innocent, yet I find you skulking in gardens and darkened rooms, and you drink brandy. Hardly the kind of behaviors one would expect from a well-bred young woman."

"I didn't drink the brandy."

"Hmm, well, that doesn't excuse your other personality flaws, does it?"

"Personality flaws? I'll have you know that I'm one of the nicest people in the world. Sweet, kind, generous—everyone says so." Eugenie was starting to get a little perturbed, and de Lacey was wickedly enjoying her discomfiture. He strolled over to stand directly in front of where she sat.

"All I've seen is a young woman who is headstrong, curiously indifferent to the rules of society, and far too nosy for her own good."

"Well!" Eugenie's color was high, now, and she bolted up, her little fists clenched. De Lacey took a lazy step back to allow her room. "If that's what you think of me, monsieur, perhaps I should remove my disgraceful presence from yours. I'm sure you would not like to continue to be sullied by one such as I." She tried to stuff her feet back into her shoes, and de Lacey watched, amused, as she could not do so, and in the end, she had to sit back down on the settee to get them on. As she jumped up again, de Lacey moved to block her.

"Not so soon, my little pea hen. I find your presence refreshing and interesting."

"As well as nosy and indifferent?" Her acidic tone brought a chuckle to his lips.

"That is as it may be. However, those flaws are well and truly covered by your loveliness and charm."

"I beg your pardon?" Eugenie couldn't hide her confusion. Indeed, de Lacey himself wondered from where the words had come. He blushed.

"It's common knowledge that you are lovely and charming, mademoiselle. I don't think I'm saying anything—how does the phrase go? —out of spin there."

"Do you mean 'out of turn'?" A whisper of a smile passed over Eugenie's lips, and de Lacey saw the amusement return to her eyes.

Eugenie walked to the door. "Now, I do believe it would be appropriate if I were to exit this room, monsieur, and creep back to the ballroom. You see? I certainly do understand the proprieties involved."

"I did not say you didn't understand them, mademoiselle. I said you had a strange disregard for them."

"Maybe it would be better to say I prefer my own rules to those thrust upon me. For example, I do not find it surprising that I should want to know more of the gentleman who interests me." She blushed a little as de Lacey raised one eyebrow.

"What if such knowledge led to loss of admiration or affection for the gentleman in question?" he asked gravely.

She grinned to herself. "I am not certain that could still occur," she admitted under her breath, "however, there are some questions that simply cannot be asked within the confines of polite society, and yet I need to know the answers before I... before I..." She flushed becomingly. "You see? The rules forbid me to say exactly what I mean."

"You do understand those rules are there for your protection, *hein*?"

Eugenie released a puff of a sigh. "Well, to tell you the truth, I do find the rules quite constricting. It was different in Paris."

She looked off into the distance and said the words with such deep longing that de Lacey's heart went out to her. He knew what she meant. England, with all its modernity and industry and propriety, could simply never shape up to the country that they both loved. He moved smoothly toward her and placed his arms around her, a comforting, brotherly gesture.

"I know," he said. "Life has turned upside down for us, hasn't it?"

"These restrictions are so very difficult to fit in with."

"More so for you than for me, but I do understand."

"And I haven't heard any news of my *papa* at all. It's most frustrating." She tipped her head back to look at him. He couldn't help but notice the tears sparkling in her eyes.

"Eugenie," he breathed, just before he lowered his lips to hers.

CHAPTER EIGHTEEN

Eugenie felt every part of her body spark to life at his touch, even as her mind shouted an unheeded warning. De Lacey pulled her close, and she extricated her arms from his embrace so she could throw them around his neck, her fingers threading into his hair. She didn't understand the feelings that de Lacey brought out in her, but she knew without a doubt that she wanted to feel them all, that she wanted to experience everything de Lacey could offer.

Eugenie could feel the hard planes of his body through their clothing—his strong, muscular chest and the firmness of his thighs, as well as something she couldn't quite identify between them—oh! She realized what it was, and flushed, even as her kisses grew more eager.

De Lacey broke the kiss, but only to sweep Eugenie on to a nearby couch, half laying her down and covering her body with his before he resumed kissing her. He had moved from her mouth and was dropping tiny, hot kisses on her jaw and neck, working his way down to her décolletage.

Eugenie's breath came short and sharp as her skin sizzled where de Lacey touched the edge of her dress where her silky breasts were hidden. He allowed one lazy finger to dip beneath the fabric, and his feather touch had her grounding out a tortured whisper, "More."

She didn't know these feelings of pleasure and torture and want, like a cloud of confusing passion they encircled her until she forgot everything and everyone except the man stretched above her.

"I love you," she whispered, so quietly that even she couldn't quite hear it.

De Lacey started, then continued his kisses, murmuring, "I love you too, *chérie*."

But something in his tone brought Eugenie's cloudy thoughts back into focus. She struggled to sit up.

"What is it, *mon cœur*?" de Lacey asked, stopping his kisses but continuing to stroke her from the side of her face, down her neck, across her shoulder, and down her arm.

Eugenie shivered. "You just said you love me."

"What of it, Eugenie?"

"Do you? Do you really?"

"Right now, *ma chérie*, I love you more than any other woman in the world." He made a movement as if to continue his kisses, but she stopped him with one raised hand.

"Right now? But what about after? What about later? Will you still love me then?"

De Lacey flapped a hand. "Love is such a misused word, Eugenie. How does one define it?" He sat back, seeming to realize their lovemaking session was suspended, for at least a short while. To Eugenie, he appeared bored, which sparked her anger.

"So, for you, love is merely a fleeting emotion?"

"Of course. Love doesn't last. And when it does, all it does is cause heartache and unfulfilled longing." While his words held a note of regret, he seemed to stop and reflect on them for a moment, and Eugenie was curious all over again.

"It sounds as if you have loved and lost, monsieur."

"It is not a subject I wish to discuss with you, mademoiselle."

Eugenie was stung by his words and his tone, which had turned hard.

"Why not? I am a grown woman. I am able to hold a rational conversation, and it is a subject I am vitally interested in since it would appear I have made the mistake of falling in love with you."

He let out a short bark of laughter. "A grown woman, are you?

Let me ask you this." He moved in as close as he could to her, laying his arm across the back of the settee behind her. "Have you ever had the breath taken from your body by a kiss that you thought had stolen your very soul? Have you known loss so deep that you cannot see the bottom of the well, yet you allow yourself to slide toward the oblivion, regardless of the consequences? Have you ever woken up in a foreign bed in a foreign land and not known for a moment if you were alive or dead? Have you felt the touch of a lover on your flesh, awakening all desire in your bones, and then, have you lost all that you desire through your own foolish pride?" His voice, so close to her ear, tickled the sensitive hairs on the organ and made her lift her shoulder just a little.

"Teach me," she said breathlessly, her eyes shining brightly. "Teach me all that you know of love so that I would know it too."

He kissed her then, hard and driving, pushing her back against the settee, both of his hands grasping her breasts through her gown, kneading the soft, pliant flesh. Eugenie moaned, deep in her throat, lifting her pelvis to meet his. Then he made a little irritated sound and pulled away, his breathing sharp.

"I cannot."

"Cannot what, monsieur?" The loss of his lips left her a little despondent.

"Teach you. Not like this. I won't despoil you. And I can't afford a mistress, Eugenie."

"I don't seek to be your mistress."

"What then?"

She blushed. "Are you going to make me say it out loud?"

"Yes."

"Very well then." She stood up, took a deep breath and crossed her arms over her chest. "I wish to marry you." Before he could respond, she added, "However, I won't marry you unless you love me with a... a grand passion. Which means me, and only me. Forever."

His eyebrow raised, and Eugenie thought she heard him choke just a little before he replied, "I beg your pardon? A grand passion?"

"Yes. It is important to me that my husband love only me. And if that is to occur, he must love me with a grand passion."

"That is a little overly romantic is it not, Eugenie?"

Eugenie shook her head, not noticing the vicomte's use of her first name. "No, I have thought long about the matter. It is not romantic. It is a practicality that I require to ensure my happiness." She sat back down beside him, folding her hands in her lap and blushing. "I suppose you think me foolish."

De Lacey's expression suggested just that, but he said in a modulated tone, "Of course not. I am simply unsure that I can meet such a stringent condition."

She looked enquiringly at him, and he continued, taking Eugenie's cold hand in both of his warm ones. "You do me honor, Mademoiselle Ponnette. I too, wish to marry you. You are fresh and delightful and… I have a growing fondness for you."

Eugenie's dazzling smile seemed to light the room better than the glow of the fire. Then, as the words sunk in, she frowned.

"But you don't love me?" Her voice was small and forlorn. He tipped her head up so that he could look into her eyes.

"I love you, in that I wish to protect and honor and care for you. I like you, as a person and I think you will make a lovely viscountess. But I don't love you with a grand passion."

"Could you ever love me like that—with a grand passion?"

De Lacey frowned. Eugenie could see that he was giving the question serious contemplation.

"I don't know, *chérie*. I…"

"It is alright," she replied. "Perhaps all we need to do is work further to develop your grand passion."

One corner of de Lacey's mouth lifted upward in a smile. "Perhaps we do."

She stood up, brushing down her gown, trying to repair the creases that had formed. "But perhaps not now. Now I should leave the room before we are discovered. I fear honor would be a fleeting thing if we were found here together, especially seated in each other's arms on the settee." She hoped he would pull her back, but to her disappointment, he agreed.

"I suspect you are right, *chérie*." He too stood, and went to the door, easing it open and peeping out. "There is nobody on the landing at the moment, so if you creep back downstairs, I will join you in a few minutes."

Eugenie brushed past him on the way out the door, rising on tiptoes to meet his lips as she did. Molten fire raced through her veins, and she was sure she saw it flare up in de Lacey's eyes as well.

Perhaps… just perhaps, she could inspire him to a grand passion.

Unseen, Eugenie returned to the ballroom, rejoining Felicity.

"Where have you been?" Felicity scolded. "I have had to tell three different gentlemen that you were taking care of a personal matter, and I told an out-and-out falsehood to your Aunt."

"Aunt Lucinda? Where is she? I should go and speak to her."

"No, you should tell me what you found out." Felicity grabbed her arm. "And you're going nowhere until you do so."

Eugenie smiled. "I found out that he wants to marry me."

Felicity's mouth dropped open. "How on earth did you find that out?"

"I asked him."

"You asked him?"

"Yes. Well, he forced me to ask him."

Felicity frowned. "My goodness, now I'm confused. Was this in front of Lord Edenburgh? For it seems quite a burden to place on a lady, under the circumstances."

"No, Lord Edenburgh had exited the room by then."

"You were in the room with him alone?" Felicity seemed truly shocked, but Eugenie waved her concerns away.

"Since I'm going to marry him anyway, it was really neither here nor there."

"That's not true, Eugenie. Imagine if someone had discovered you. Your reputation would never recover."

Eugenie clicked her fingers. "Pah! I give that for reputation."

"Well, perhaps you should treat it with more respect," replied Felicity. "After all, your precious vicomte could still walk away you know. There has been no formal offer."

Eugenie smiled tightly, knowing that her friend was right, but not willing to concede the point. "Thank you for your consideration, *mon amie*. I appreciate it. Now, I should really go and find my Aunt."

"Wait. You still didn't tell me if you discovered his secret?"

Eugenie's face dropped into a frown. "No, I didn't."

"So, it's still possible that he's doing something nefarious?"

"I suppose so." Eugenie spoke the words slowly. "However, I wonder if it is even that much of a concern?"

"Really? Oh, my poor Eugenie.".

"What?"

"Why, you've gone and fallen in love with your vicomte haven't you?"

"Of course I have. I want to marry him."

"No, I mean really fallen in love with him."

Eugenie shook her head. "I don't understand the question."

Felicity tucked her arm under Eugenie's. "For all your French sophistication, you really are a peagoose when it comes to love, aren't you? Do you blush when he crosses the room? Do you feel things in your body when he gets close? Do you seek him out in a crowd of people?"

"Yes."

"Then, my dear, you have fallen in love with him."

Eugenie pondered Felicity's words for a moment; then a smile spread across her face. "Well, in that case, I suppose I have."

"It's not necessarily a good thing, you know."

"Oh? Why is that?"

"Mama tells me that many marriages based on love are troublesome from the beginning, with the wife wishing her husband to spend all his time at her side, and the husband, wishing to be anywhere but there. She wears out his love by doting on him and hanging off him, and eventually, the gentleman tires of this and seeks comfort in the arms of another."

Eugenie scoffed. "Are you certain this wasn't just a tale your mother told you to scare you away from a love match?"

"No, this was a cautionary tale she read to me from Lady Finicky's Book of Modes of Behavior.

"Lady Finicky?" Eugenie quirked a brow at Felicity, who flushed.

"Of course, everybody knows that the name Lady Finicky is a nom de plume. However, the advice is very practical and helpful."

"Well, it seems to me that your Lady Finicky has forgotten one important thing."

"What's that?"

"That sometimes, husbands are also in love with their wives. And in my case, I have made that very clear to the vicomte."

"What have you made clear?"

"That I will accept nothing but a grand passion."

Felicity stopped for a moment and closed her eyes. "Do you mean to tell me that you told Vicomte Landreville that he must have a grand passion for you before you will marry him?"

"Of course."

"And he agreed to this?"

"Well, let's say we are working further on it. Felicity, you know I can't marry otherwise. I am a far too sensitive woman to marry a man who does not love me. I'm certain I can bring the vicomte around to my way of thinking. "She bestowed a lovely smile on her friend. "And now, I simply must go to my Aunt, before she has an apoplexy—I'm certain she thinks I am up to no good just as soon as she turns her back."

"As well she might," murmured Felicity under her breath, shaking her head at Eugenie's words.

Eugenie threw her a strange look, but fluttered away, in search of her Aunt.

"If only I could be as certain as she," Felicity sighed, turning back to the party and then she startled. "Goodness." The earl was standing right there, holding two glasses of orgeat.

"I had thought you and Mademoiselle Ponnette might appreciate a drink, Lady Felicity, but it seems I am too late to minister to your friend's needs."

"Never mind," replied Felicity cheerfully. "I'll take one of the glasses, and you can drink the second."

"Me? Drink orgeat?" He shuddered. "Revolting stuff. Mother used to make me drink it when I was younger."

"Well, maybe you can just hold it and pretend to be drinking it," Felicity offered, and the earl accepted her suggestion with a nod and a smile.

"Now, shall we sit for a moment and have a nice chat?" He gave her a conspiratorial smile. "I have to say, the reason I came over was to get away from the damned debutantes. It gets to be a bit of a chore after a while. Come. Sit." The earl took Felicity's arm and led her to a nearby set of chairs, tall and wide with comfortable padding.

The earl handed Felicity into hers first, then lowered himself into the other, sighing with relief. "Ah, now, that's better. My poor feet have been stood on all day—it is heaven indeed to be able to step off them for a short while."

"Indeed," replied Felicity, staring down into her orgeat. Now that she was seated with the earl, she didn't quite know what to say. Quincey was an old playmate, but the Earl of Edenburgh was a terrifying prospect.

The earl leaned over to pat her on the knee. "Don't worry, Lady Felicity, I'm not here to terrorize you." At her sudden protestation, he put a hand up, shaking his head. "You can't fool me. You were hoping I wasn't going to launch into one of my political speeches or recite some poetry."

Felicity smiled. "I think I can unequivocally say I did not expect you to break out into poetry, my Lord. I don't think I even knew you read poetry."

"No, I don't," replied the earl, leaning in close and beckoning Felicity in closer. "But if I did, the works of Wordsworth would rather outshine those of the earlier metaphysical poets."

"You are a fan of Wordsworth, then?" Felicity replied, delighted.

"I will admit a fondness for his prose." The earl smiled at Felicity. "You see? How long have we known each other, Lady

Felicity, and still I can surprise you?"

She laughed gently. "Indeed, you can, my Lord. Indeed, you can."

Eugenie hooked her arm in her Aunt's, but before her aunt could scold, she whispered in her ear, "Is it my imagination, or are Lord Edenburgh and Lady Felicity looking rather cozy over there in the corner?"

"Where?" Aunt Lucinda, always on the lookout for a new piece of gossip, swiveled her head around until she spied them out. "They are a lovely couple," she said, only a hint of malice in her tone. "He, becoming portly and balding, and she, never going to be of the first water. They would make a good match."

"I think they would make an excellent match," declared Eugenie, still watching them. "I think they just don't know it yet."

Her Aunt looked sharply at Eugenie. "You have no plans to assist them on their way do you, Eugenie? I would counsel against it."

"How so?"

"These things will work themselves out if they are to be. They don't need a young busybody coming in and spoiling the natural workings of time."

Eugenie didn't necessarily agree, but she did hold her tongue. And the distraction of seeing Felicity with the earl, and the urgent need to speak to all of her cronies about it, allowed Eugenie to get away without having to tell her aunt where she had been. Goodness knows what she would say if she knew Eugenie had been closeted in a private room with a gentleman!

Eugenie thought back to de Lacey's kisses, those scorching, drugged moments of bliss. Her own breathlessness at being caught up in his arms, and his scent surrounding her, intoxicating her. His whispers of passion and need and want circling around in her head.

Such a gentleman must be capable of a grand passion. Of that, Eugenie was certain.

But how was she to persuade the vicomte of it? And that his

grand passion should be for her?

CHAPTER NINETEEN

The following afternoon, Eugenie battled again with Felicity, this time in the privacy of her bedchamber, and for a much different reason.

"It will be easy," she insisted. "We say we are going to the lending library, then instead, we go to see Mr. Smythe."

"A thief taker." Felicity pressed her lips into a fine line. "I do believe your obsession with your vicomte has given you brain fever."

"Nonsense. I just want to know what secret he is hiding. After all, if I am to marry him, I should know everything about him, *hein*?"

"Maybe sometimes it's better for couples to have some secrets," said Felicity. "You know, to add mystery and a little spice to the relationship."

"Not me," replied Eugenie forcefully. "I want to know everything there is to know about my vicomte."

Felicity was just as forceful. "But we can't go visiting a thief taker, Eugenie. It wouldn't be proper."

"That is why we will go in disguise, *ma chérie*. No one will even know it was us. Except, of course, Mr. Smythe."

"And just who is this Mr. Smythe? Where do you know him from?"

"I found his name on an advertisement in the Times." Eugenie's words were airy. However, a flush came to her cheek.

"From the Times? Eugenie!"

"I couldn't exactly walk up to my aunt and uncle and ask them, could I? Nor anyone else of my acquaintance? Do you really think they would give me the direction of their most trusted thief taker? No, they'd more likely have me thrown into Bedlam."

"Perhaps that's where you belong," said Felicity under her breath, glaring at Eugenie.

"Come on, Felicity," Eugenie said in a wheedling tone. "It will be an adventure."

"Humph." Felicity crossed her arms. "For you maybe. I shall be scared to death the whole time."

"But you will do it for me because I'm your best friend and you love me?" Eugenie turned all her charm on to her friend, opening her blue eyes wide and giving her the most beguiling smile she could make.

Felicity sighed. "Fine. I'll go with you. But where are we going to get disguises?"

"I already have my lady's maid, Rachel, working on that. She has a sister who owns a second-hand clothing store."

"Second-hand clothing! Eugenie, don't tell me you expect me to wear someone else's clothing?"

"Felicity, don't be so precious. They will have been laundered you know."

"But they've been on somebody else's body." Felicity shuddered.

"I know! Is it not exciting? While we are walking along, we can make up stories about the previous owners of our clothing."

With much beguiling, Eugenie managed to have Felicity agree to meet her the following day.

Address in hand, Eugenie strode up to the door of Mr. Harry Smythe's office, a terrified Felicity creeping along beside her. Sadly, however, she didn't feel as confident as she looked, even though their disguises were brilliant. Rachel had found somber gray dresses, at least three years out of fashion, and heavy veils to cover their faces.

She stepped inside to be met by a man she assumed was a clerk, even though he was a big, burly fellow with a nose that had obviously been broken more than once, and no neck to speak of.

Felicity looked up at him, mouth open and eyes goggling. Eugenie nudged her sharply in the ribs, and she shut her mouth, though she continued to stare at the enormous man.

"Can I help you?" he said in a voice that started somewhere down deep inside his cavernous chest and came out as a deep rumble. He didn't smile or make any other effort to seek the ladies' comfort, and Eugenie's nerve very nearly failed her.

But, then she remembered her mission, and her spirits revived.

"I'm here to see Mr. Smythe. I have an appointment."

"You are?"

"Miss Harrison."

"Wait here."

The brute lumbered off, and Felicity whispered in Eugenie's ear, "On my honor, I've never seen such a frightening man. We should go home, Eugenie, before we get into trouble."

"Nonsense," replied Eugenie in a rallying tone. "Now that we are here, we should definitely go through with it."

Felicity only moaned and clung tighter to Eugenie's arm.

The brute returned. "Follow me." Then he turned and went back the way he came.

Eugenie followed him, dragging Felicity along with her. Her friend was almost a dead weight as if her own legs wouldn't carry her.

To Eugenie's surprise, they ended up in a bright room at the end of the corridor. A middle-aged, respectable looking man behind a desk looked up.

"Miss Harrison, is it? Thank you, Bilge. You may go."

The brute disappeared again as Mr. Smythe came around the desk and cordially shook their hands, ushering the two of them into seats.

"Do sit down ladies. May I get you anything? Tea? Wine?"

They both shook their heads, Eugenie sitting elegantly and Felicity practically falling into the chairs by Mr. Smythe's desk. He sat down on the other side. Eugenie was surprised to find he seemed a well-spoken man, with dark hair, brushed back off his face the way a lawyer's clerk might wear it.

"So. What brings two obviously well bred young ladies to my office this fine afternoon?" He templed his fingers and smiled encouragingly.

Eugenie pulled her veil back, took a deep breath and expelled it before starting to explain. "You see, there is a gentleman I believe wishes to further his acquaintance with me. However, I came across a question about his character recently, and I was hoping you, Mr. Smythe, could follow him for a few days and discover what his secret is." Gasping a little, Eugenie sat back in her chair.

"Interesting," replied Mr. Smythe. "It's not my usual type of work, as you probably already know."

"Yes, I understand you usually seek out thieves and reap the rewards for their capture."

"Indeed. So how did you think to pay me for following this fellow around?"

"I have quite a bit of pin money."

Felicity's head shot up, and she looked at Eugenie warningly. Eugenie looked at her questioningly as Felicity shook her head.

Mr. Smythe, who watched the exchange, laughed. "I do believe your friend is trying to warn you not to disclose exactly how much pin money you have, Miss Harrison. You see, people in my business are mostly crooks and thieves themselves, out to get as much money as they can, so my fees would, in a strange turn of events, exactly match the money you have available." Turning to Felicity, he said, "Is that not so, Miss?"

Felicity colored deeply and scowled at Mr. Smythe. "It's my lady," she muttered under her breath.

"Please believe that I am not out to dun you, Mademoiselle Ponnette."

Eugenie and Felicity gasped.

"How do you know who I am?"

Mr. Smythe smiled. "What kind of a thief taker would I be if I couldn't even deduce the identity of the clients who wish to avail themselves of my services?"

Finally, Felicity spoke, her voice shaking. "You will not tell anyone of our whereabouts, will you, Mr. Smythe? It would be a terrible scandal."

"Client confidentiality is a necessity in my line of work don't you know? Now, please tell me a little more about this gentleman. Am I right to assume it is Vicomte Landreville you seek information on?"

Again, Eugenie was amazed. "*Oui*, it is he."

In ten minutes, Eugenie had spilled the entire story to Mr. Smythe, ably assisted with details by Felicity, who had now found her tongue. Mr. Smythe, to his credit, listened closely to the two young ladies, taking some notes, and showing a strong interest in the story.

"Will you take the case, sir?" asked Eugenie.

"Yes, of course," replied Mr. Smythe with a smile. "It will be a pleasure to follow a gentleman rather than the usual rabble I am accustomed to. I should be pleased to forward you a report of my findings in, say, two weeks?"

"Two weeks? So soon? I imagined you would need to follow him for months to get a good idea."

"Allow me to let you in on a little secret, my dear." Mr. Smythe beckoned them, and they leaned forward eagerly. "It's only difficult to follow someone when they know they are being followed. In those cases, one must employ disguise and subterfuge, so the target doesn't realize they are being followed. Someone who doesn't know—well, it's just a matter of walking along behind them to see where they go."

Eugenie nodded.

They agreed on a price for the transaction—Eugenie had no idea what the going rate was for shadowing another person, so she agreed to Mr. Smythe's first offer—and with the promise of a missive being delivered in a sennight, they were once again ushered out on to the street by the enormous Bilge.

Eugenie felt a little let down by the whole transaction. Mr. Smythe seemed too kindly and sympathetic and just too... plainly normal to be a thief taker. He was supposed to be mysterious, with a hint of danger lurking about him. Mr. Smythe was more like a jolly shopkeeper, or the father of a whole tribe of fat children.

They hurried to the carriage which eventually deposited them at the kitchen door, and where Rachel waited with cloaks to cover their strange clothing so they could get upstairs without drawing attention. They changed back into their regular attire, and Felicity prepared to leave.

"Eugenie, I never wish to be involved in one of your schemes again, do you understand? I've never been so scared in my life! Goodbye, my dear. I suppose I'll see you tonight?"

"Of course, *mon amie*." Eugenie was all contrition, but her eyes sparkled with mischief. "Never again."

Felicity sighed, shook her head and left with a smile.

Now all Eugenie could do was wait.

CHAPTER TWENTY

"She will only have me if I agree to a grand passion for her."

De Lacey paced around the boudoir, not noticing the small smile that crossed her face. She went to the drinks cart and poured them both a large shot of brandy. De Lacey downed his in one gulp, before handing the glass back to her with a wry smile.

"Do you know what the foolish part is?"

"What is that?"

"I believe it would be possible."

Her fine brows rose in amazement. "Truly? You could love this little woman?"

"Not only could. I do love her. Somehow." De Lacey seemed frustrated as if he couldn't quite understand what he was feeling. "It's like… I feel something for her I've never felt, and it's more than just the desire to bed her or to enjoy her company. I want to protect her. When she tells me of her problems, I want to shield her from them, like some kind of… unenlightened baboon. When she is in a room, I seek her out. In the beginning, I merely watched her, but now, I all but run across the room to be beside her. I want to know her opinions, her thoughts, her feelings."

"So, she engages you intellectually?"

"Yes, but that's not it either." He tapped his lip with his finger. "I feel like I'm a better person with her." De Lacey looked up into her eyes and blushed, shrugging his shoulders. "I sound like a fool."

"No, Jean, you sound like a man who, perhaps for the first time in his life, is actually falling in love."

He shook his head. "But how can I offer Eugenie a grand passion if I don't know myself that this feeling will last? It could be fleeting. It could dissipate the first moment after I bed her. And then what? I will have trapped her into marriage under false pretenses." He reflected for a moment. "And what about the money? She will think I have only married her to get my hands on her fortune. Which I actually am doing. I still need her money." He dropped into a chair and placed his head into his hands. "She must hate me."

She laughed. "Oh, my dear, listen to yourself. You may not be totally in love with Mademoiselle Ponnette just yet. However, you are sailing very close to the wind." He looked a little confused, and she continued. "Your concern is more about the damage it may do to her, rather than yourself, were you to end up in a loveless marriage. It's precious." She allowed the smile to slip from her face as she sat down. They were silent for a moment, lost in their own thoughts before she spoke again.

"Perhaps it's time for you to stop coming to see me, Jean."

He looked up at her swiftly from under drawn brows, studying her face, then slowly nodding.

"Perhaps it is." He gazed at her hair for a moment.

"We probably can't remain friends, Jean," she whispered.

He reached out to take her hand. "I hope we can, for your wise counsel has never failed me. You know, I've cut off all contact with that other girl from Kent after taking your advice."

"Really? How did she take it?"

"Not particularly well," he admitted with a short chuckle. "I received a mighty dressing down, but at least now I am free of her."

"That's good," she replied with a nod. "It was always going to be a sticky situation to get out of."

"Indeed. Which is why I am glad to be rid of her."

Her smile wavered. "And now, rid of me too."

"Never that, *chérie*. You are too good a friend to be rid of me."

She smiled, but it was sad. "That's just a pleasant dream, Jean, and you know it."

He dropped her hand and rose from his chair. "Why should it be? I can acknowledge you in public. We can still converse."

"But it will hardly be the same, will it?"

De Lacey's frown was deep now; his green eyes almost lost under his drawn brows. "How I hate these strictures. I can meet Quincey wherever I like, and whenever I like with not a word being said. But you?"

"But I must ever be kept at arm's length, my dear. As it should be, if you carry a grand passion for your Mademoiselle Ponnette."

"It's just not right."

"Perhaps not, but it is what it is."

"I don't like it."

"I don't see another way around it." She reached out, and he took both of her hands. She rose to stand. "My dear, what we've had, it was wonderful, but it's time to say *adieu*." Wrapping her arms around his shoulders, she pulled him close. "I'll never forget you, Jean."

He hugged her in return, his arms strong around her back. "I don't want it to end this way," he muttered into her shoulder.

"The end was always going to be difficult," she replied in a whisper.

With an oath, de Lacey tore himself out of her arms and without looking back, walked out the door.

She let her tears flow freely. There would never be another quite like Jean de Lacey.

CHAPTER TWENTY-ONE

As the days and weeks of the season flashed by, de Lacey and Tatillion grew more and more bold in their endeavors to interrupt the trade of the Waldershare Gang. They held up several carts and small vehicles around the same vicinity on the London Road, cheerfully relieving the gang of their precious cargo while ignoring the men's threats and accusations. They managed to put a sizeable dent in proceedings, enough that whenever de Lacey encountered Arthur at The Ancient Crow, there was a scowl on his craggy face and a new curse on the heads of the robbers. All efforts to apprehend the robbers had failed. And Arthur was becoming a little desperate.

De Lacey didn't know what Tatillion did with the supplies they liberated, and he didn't want to know. However, he was unsurprised to find a new white shirt amongst his belonging and a steady supply of fine, French brandy to his rooms.

De Lacey silently toasted his success while seated with Lord Edenburgh in the convivial surroundings of Brooks's. Of course, the earl, contentedly puffing away on his pipe and reading the current edition of The Times, had no notion that his companion was a wicked highwayman, and de Lacey had every intention of keeping it that way. Even though the earl accepted his share of contraband, he was still a magistrate, and de Lacey didn't want to put any strain on their easy friendship.

He had been surprised to discover he felt no nagging guilt or conscience because of his escapades. While they certainly frightened the men they robbed, they did not injure anyone except in a fair fight, and smuggled goods were, as far as de Lacey was concerned, fair game. Quite apart from that, he was not considering a career as a robber. It was merely a means to an end, with an end in sight.

He and Tatillion planned to rob a much larger coach in a few day's time that carried even more luxury—silks and lace, French ornaments and small furniture pieces. These would fetch a pretty penny for the Waldershare Gang on the black market, for such items were in extremely short supply due to the war. The goods were arriving on a ship from Holland which was docking in two days. The Waldershare Gang would be out in full force to clear the goods from the ship, and then many coaches and a large number of horses and men would be pressed into service, many a farmer asked to leave his barn door ajar. For their compliance, the household would be kept in tea and spirits in a grand way.

De Lacey hoped that this step up to a larger target would force Arthur's hand, bring his deception out into the open, and free him of the gang. A smile crossed his face at the thought of the weight that would be removed from his shoulders, and the delectable prize that awaited him in the form of Eugenie Ponnette when he succeeded.

"You certainly appear to be in good spirits today," remarked Lord Edenburgh through a cloud of smoke from his favorite pipe.

"Do I?" De Lacey couldn't keep the satisfaction out of his voice.

"Yes, sitting there smiling away to yourself."

"*Mon ami*, things are finally starting to look rosy for me," he said, unable to keep the smugness from his tone.

"Oh? How so?"

De Lacey leaned back in his winged chair with a contented sigh. "The fair Mademoiselle Ponnette will soon be mine, and all of my worries will be over."

The earl laughed far too heartily over de Lacey's words. De Lacey threw him a glare of irritation, which only made his friend chuckle all the more until de Lacey was preparing to be offended.

"Oh, my dear fellow, you will be the death of me," he cried, wiping his eyes. "All of your worries will be over? You will have a wife. All of your worries are just beginning."

De Lacey smiled. "Very well, *mon ami*, let us say my current worries will be over, to be replaced with a worry that I am happy to accept."

"Happy?"

The grin de Lacey sent at his friend was genuine, almost youthful. "Extremely happy."

"Interesting." His lordship took a reflective puff on his pipe. "Whatever happened to the old de Lacey—the one who used to bed three women in a night and be awake at eight the following morning to brag about it?"

"He is gone, *mon ami*," replied de Lacey airily, "to be replaced by the sober, settled gentleman you see before you."

The earl harrumphed, sending a puff of fragrant smoke into the air. "Ten to one you tire of Mademoiselle Ponnette within a sennight."

"Done," replied de Lacey promptly, then he smiled again. "Ah but you see, Quincey, it is a bet I cannot lose. Mademoiselle Ponnette excites in me all the old urges, but also some new, interesting ones that I have been led to believe are the markers of true love."

Lord Edenburgh snorted. "Really?" he drawled. "I'll be glad to discuss them further with you two weeks after your wedding, when you are here, tearing your hair out and handing over my winnings."

"It will not happen," replied de Lacey firmly.

"Still, I will make that bet."

De Lacey scowled. It did not sit well with him that his old friend believed him incapable of love. He wanted to try to explain what he was feeling, to make the earl understand, only he knew he would come across like a love-struck fool.

To de Lacey, a shroud of ill-will settled over the pair of them, although the earl didn't seem to notice. Quincey continued to puff away on his pipe, his eyes on the newspaper, oblivious to the storm of emotions he had unleashed in de Lacey's breast. Didn't he realize this was a momentous event? He took a quick, dissatisfied sip of his brandy, trying to decide whether he would make a fool of himself if only to make his friend understand. Thankfully, at that moment, the earl decided to change the subject.

"Oh, de Lacey, I need you to attend a card party I'm throwing on Thursday."

Thursday was when he and Tatillion would be holding up the London-bound coach. He wondered if Lord Edenburgh was testing him. De Lacey glanced up at his friend from under his lowered brows, only to find the earl hadn't even looked up from his paper.

"*Mon ami*, it will be impossible," he said, presenting his hands and shrugging in typical French gesture. "I am previously engaged."

At this, the earl looked up. "But you must attend. We need the excuse to decline to attend Mrs. Wilberforce's coming out party for her disagreeable daughter." Lord Edenburgh raised an eyebrow even as he raised his brandy glass to his lips. "Please don't tell me you are planning to attend? Alice Wilberforce is fat and frumpy and has a hideous squint. Surely you wouldn't give up your court of Miss Ponnette for such a prize?"

"I already told you, Quincey, I am going to marry Mademoiselle Ponnette. I'll certainly not be giving her up, and definitely not for Alice Wilberforce."

"Then what are you doing, old man? I didn't think there were any other entertainments on Thursday."

De Lacey should have been able to list off a half-dozen events that he could have attended, but right at that moment, his mind went blank.

"I...thought I'd just stay at home that evening," he replied, knowing the weak excuse wouldn't deter Lord Edenburgh.

"Nonsense. I need you to make up the second fourth. A night at home? Who ever heard of such a thing? No, no, you will attend."

"I'm sorry my friend, it cannot happen." De Lacey's firm tone brought his friend's usually dull glance into sharp focus.

"Do you have as assignation?"

"No. I do not. Certainly not, when I am pursuing Mademoiselle Ponnette." De Lacey sighed inwardly. He was seized with the sudden temptation to tell Lord Edenburgh all about his circumstances, and his task for Thursday, but he shook off the temptation. His friend's morals were perhaps a little fluid. Still, de Lacey did not think he would be able to overlook such an enormous transgression. So, he fabricated an excuse.

"Very well, my friend, you have found me out. I am... meeting some low acquaintances for a bawdy night." He stared back at the earl, one eyebrow raised, as if inviting his friend to suggest he was lying.

Instead, the earl said mildly, "That is unlike you, de Lacey. I had thought you only appeared in the highest of circles."

"Well, people change, Quincey. I've changed. You've changed."

"Me?"

"Yes, with your paunch and your fondness for politics and your fastidiousness. Nothing like the carefree gentleman you used to be."

"Ah, but you see, intrinsically I am the same. I still hold myself to higher principles than the rabble. I am still careful of my acquaintance. And," at this Lord Edenburgh frowned, "if I remember correctly, I've always been fastidious in my dress. It was one of the things you used to tease me mercilessly about."

De Lacey had to chuckle. As younger men, they had traveled part of the continent together, and it was true, Quincey—at that time Viscount Healey—had always striven to follow the highest of fashions, to limited success and the constant amusement of his companion.

"However, that still doesn't excuse you from my card party. I simply must insist that you attend."

"And I simply must insist that I cannot." De Lacey sat back in his chair and crossed his arms in front of him.

The earl sighed. "I will be eaten up with curiosity until I find out what you are up to, my friend."

"Maybe that will take care of some of your paunch," replied de

Lacey, "for I will not be telling you."

Lord Edenburgh regarded him over his brandy glass, from which he took a sip. "I do wonder if you are up to something nefarious, you know."

"Yes, I suppose you do."

They engaged in a silent battle of wills, staring each other down until the earl broke eye contact with a laugh. "Very well, don't tell me. I don't really care anyway."

De Lacey was chilled by his tone. He knew the earl was going to start digging around for information that very day. He needed to complete this smuggling business, and fast.

CHAPTER TWENTY-TWO

Two weeks dragged as painfully as Eugenie had ever known, despite the constant round of balls, soirees, and engagements. She looked for de Lacey everywhere she went and, when she saw him, every fear she had concerning his secrets fell aside. She was sure de Lacey was happy to see her as well. He seemed lighter somehow, maybe even younger.

But there were also those times when he was not in attendance. During those times, Eugenie feared for him, feared for what he was doing that was so secretive he wouldn't even confess to her. Each time he returned, she railed against him, insisting he tell her where he had been. But it didn't matter how infuriated Eugenie was, or how much she shouted and raged; he refused to let her in on his secret.

And now, Mr. Smythe's report had arrived.

Eugenie sat on her bed and stared at the fat envelope in front of her. Now that the moment had come, and she was about to know de Lacey's secrets, she was afraid—afraid to look at it, afraid of what it might contain, of what the contents might mean for her.

She had no doubts about de Lacey's desire to wed her; she was in love with him, and she was sure that he was falling. The stolen kisses and words of endearment that he whispered in her ear when nobody else could hear were all signs of his growing affection. Surely that was enough? Did she really need to know what else he had been doing? He only kept it from her to save her from worry and concern. Wasn't that a good quality in a husband?

To ensure his wife was sheltered from the horrible things in life?

She sighed and picked up the envelope. It was heavy—at least half a dozen pages she would assume. Maybe the document comprised lists of when Mr. Smythe or his employees followed de Lacey around, tracking his every move, checking into his deepest, darkest secrets. Did she really want to know?

Or maybe, the document would tell her that de Lacey had no secret at all—that he had tried to make himself more interesting when in fact his time away was spent at a special bootmaker in Hertfordshire because he simply couldn't get his boots made as well anywhere else. Or something just as trite.

She sighed. She knew it wasn't that. But she had no idea what it would be either. And that was what frightened her. What if it turned out that he was a murderer, or had another wife, or frequented bawdy houses? What then?

Enough, Eugenie. Open the envelope.

She took her letter opener from her pocket and with a deep breath, she slit the envelope and pulled out the pages.

The first one was a covering letter, very polite, telling her the job was complete and that there was a bill and a report attached. She put that page to the back, along with the second page that itemized the bill.

She scanned the first page of the report. As expected, it listed times and dates over the past weeks where Mr. Smythe had followed de Lacey—mainly to Brooks's and back to his lodgings on Jermyn Street, but every now and then to balls and soirées and dinners. Eugenie herself was mentioned in the notes, at those times she had been present in de Lacey's company. She blushed, wondering if Mr. Smythe had any occasion to spy on de Lacey and herself when they were secretly meeting to share a furtive embrace?

Wait a moment—what was this?

"Wednesday, 9 April: Followed Monsieur de Lacey by carriage to The Ancient Crow, Waldershare. He met several of the taproom's people as if they were old friends. A meeting was held, in which what appeared to be plans for a heist or a smuggling operation were discussed."

Eugenie frowned. A heist or a smuggling operation? She turned the page and found another entry, for the following Friday.

"Friday 11 April: De Lacey and another man held up a carriage on its way to London. They relieved the coach of contents including brandy casks and silks."

Eugenie paled. He was a highwayman. A common thief.

It wasn't true—it couldn't be true.

"Sunday 13 April: De Lacey attended 22 Dorset Lane. Further inquiries showed this home to be owned by the current Duke of Hampshire, and is the current residence of the dowager Lady Hampshire who lives alone." So, there it was. He probably had a lover as well. Eugenie's stomach churned. Even as he was making love to her, he was involved with this slattern. She turned to the final page of the report. Mr. Smythe did not sugar coat what he thought to be the truth.

"Our inquiries into the happenings of Vicomte Landreville, Jean de Lacey lead me to conclude that he is either a highwayman or involved in a smuggling gang out of Kent. Possibly both. However, it did not appear to us that the two outcomes were connected to each other.

Additionally, there is some evidence to suggest that Vicomte Landreville may have a lover; but, the evidence collected is not enough to confirm this completely.

Our recommendation would be to pursue more information on the gentleman before you take any step of which you may come to regret."

Eugenie nodded, her blue eyes filling with tears. A Highwayman! And a lover!

She needed to get some fresh air, to process what she had discovered. She called Rachel to bring her a walking cape, boots, and hat. Rachel looked at her tear stained face with apparent concern.

"Is it a good idea to walk now, mademoiselle? You don't seem to be yourself."

"That is exactly why I need to walk now, Rachel," she replied wiping away tears.

Rachel helped her into the outdoors garments and held the door open as Eugenie stepped outside into the cool London streets.

She strode along, with Rachel a step behind her, little knowing where she was going, until she stood outside de Lacey's rooms on Jermyn Street. It was not proper for a young lady to enter those rooms—they were gentlemen's rooms, many of them single French *émigrés* like de Lacey. Still, she wanted to confront de Lacey with Mr. Smythe's findings and to insist that he explained himself.

She stared at the building for what seemed like hours, until her maid approached and said tentatively, "Mademoiselle, we should move along. We are making a spectacle of ourselves." Indeed, more than one curious glance had been thrown their way.

Eugenie allowed Rachel to lead her back to Hyde Park, to the walks where the proper ladies and gentlemen would be seen. However, she stared at the people and picturesque gardens without seeing them, so caught up was she in trying to decipher what de Lacey was doing and how it affected her. Could she overlook his misdeeds? Even if she could overlook his robbery, she could certainly not overlook his having a lover. He knew that was her one condition.

Thinking about that, invoked her anger; de Lacey *knew* she would not marry him if he had a lover. Yet, it seemed not only did he have one, but he also kept it from her, all the while smiling in her face and assuring her that she was the only one for him.

All at once, she was pushed from the side, and she heard Rachel say, "Go easy there," before her voice turned shrill. "Get your hands off my lady, or I'll report you to the magistrate."

The young woman who had intercepted Eugenie smiled as she took Eugenie's arm in a vice-like grip. "You're coming with me, my lady," she hissed in Eugenie's ear. "Now don't make a sound or I'll have to push the chiv I have poking into your lovely ribs, and I really don't want to do that."

The prick from the knife was real, and Eugenie felt a bolt of fear pass through her. But her first thought was for Rachel.

132

"All is fine, Rachel," she called back. "This is a friend of mine." In her peripheral vision, she saw Rachel nod and fall back a few steps. When she knew her maid was no longer in any danger, she turned her attention to her attacker.

"What do you want?" she asked in a haughty voice, which belied her fear and fury. The young woman just smiled, an expression that sent a shiver down Eugenie's spine.

She was hustled forward and into an old rickety coach parked a little way off the main thoroughfare. It was shabby, it's ripped silks speaking of earlier grandeur, and it smelled, of sweat and smoke and urine, all ground together into the carpets and fabrics. Eugenie curled her lip in disgust.

She tripped over the feet of another passenger, a young man who was bound, gagged and blindfolded. He wriggled in his seat, trying to speak, but the woman said, "Shut up, Jack. I don't care what you have to say."

Her abductor pushed in behind her, shouting to the driver, "Let's go, Ben."

The horses were whipped up, and Eugenie could hear Rachel screaming. She tried to get up from the seat, but was pushed roughly back down by the other woman, who pointed a wicked looking blade at her, and said, "I wouldn't do that again if I were you."

"Where are we going?" This time the fear made her voice wobble, which seemed to amuse the other woman.

"You'll see in good time. Now I'm going to blindfold and gag you. Don't fight me, if you know what's good for you. I will not hesitate to stick my chiv into your ribs."

Eugenie suffered the indignity of allowing herself to be gagged and blindfolded, choking on the filthy rag that was pushed between her teeth like a horse's bit. The woman also pitched her forward by the shoulders and tied her hands behind her back.

"Comfortable?" The sneer in the young woman's voice made Eugenie want to slap her, which of course, she couldn't. How dare this person abduct her? And for what? It wasn't as if she was an heiress or anyone of importance. She aimed a kick at in the direction of the voice, but all that did was elicit a laugh from the woman. "If you don't thrash around I'll leave your feet unbound, but if you do anything stupid, I won't hesitate to wrap you up in ropes so tight you won't be able to move an inch. You've been warned."

The young woman banged on the roof of the carriage, and it stopped. Eugenie heard the door open, and the woman said in a light, airy voice, "Enjoy the trip love," before the door closed and Eugenie could sense the young woman had left the coach. Eugenie felt the equipage sway, suggesting that the woman had swung herself up beside the driver, before she heard, "Let's go."

The coach started forward, and Eugenie was swamped with despair. A tear formed in her eye, only to be absorbed by the rag tied across her eyes.

What was she to do?

Of course, Rachel would have run back to the house to alert everyone that Eugenie had been kidnapped. Faithful Rachel, who had come with them from Paris, who had carried Isabeau the whole way. There would be trackers on her scent before she knew it.

She could sense they were heading east. Not knowing how long the journey would be, she tried to get comfortable, difficult with her hands behind her back.

She gasped as a foot touched hers—the man on the other bench! It seemed he had intended to touch her, and it offered her momentary comfort, that there was another person there, someone else to connect with, even it was in such a strange manner.

It was just a matter of waiting. Someone would rescue her. She was sure.

CHAPTER TWENTY-THREE

She was back at the Abbaye Prison, this time in the thick of the bloodshed. She saw the court set up inside the building, where the lives of her fellow Parisians were put in the balance by revolutionaries, their guilt or innocence decided upon according to whether they were friends of the republic or not.

The judges were blurry, but the faces of the prisoners were crystal clear. Some were criminals; others were thieves, counterfeiters, and murderers. They were all men, a good number of them clergy, whose only fault was to put the word of God above that of men. One by one they were judged unworthy to continue life in the earthly realm.

Instructed to leave the building via the front doors, the first of the condemned couldn't believe their luck. They dived out the door—only to be caught in a flurry of swords, clubs, and axes, cutting them down even as they thought they were escaping.

The remaining prisoners backed up, unwilling to exit. One gentleman took it upon himself to calm the condemned, announcing, "We shall face death as we faced life—unafraid and with our heads held high."

Eugenie sobbed at his bravery in the face of certain, violent death.

Rivulets of blood ran through the cobblestones where the fallen were piled up. Several men, their bodies cut to ribbons, huddled up against buildings, waiting to die, watching the blood drain from their own bodies.

Women and children ransacked the bodies of the dead and even those who were not dead but unable to fend for themselves. The bloody workers pocketed items of value, before continuing to the next body in a frenzy. And it was as she watched this final insult to the dead that she saw him, and thought her already anguished heart would break.

Her own *papa*, lying one arm thrown out, his chest and stomach crossed with wounds. His eyes were open, as was his mouth.

She walked toward him, drawn to him even as she revolted at the sight of him. Flies crawled over his face and body, and a crow landed on his chest, seeming to look him in the face before pecking at his open wounds.

Eugenie ran then, frightening the crow into flight. She picked up the limp body of her *papa*, cradling him in her arms, not noticing the blood that stained her once white dress.

"*Papa*," she sobbed, rocking him gently, the tears streaming down her face. Then, she shook him. "*Papa*, wake up. Wake up. We need you."

Despite her plea, she knew her father was dead. In horror then, she watched as his clouded eyes opened in his gray face, and he said through a mouth caked in blood, "You are stronger than you think, my daughter." When she blinked her eyes and shook her head, his eyes were closed again.

She looked around. "Somebody, help me. Help me!"

The passers by, reluctant to be associated with any of the victims, lest they themselves become targets, ignored her pleas.

The sans-culottes appeared. As before, they were armed, their eyes empty. They moved as one, dragging their implements of destruction along the ground, the scraping sound dulled by the blood that clung to them.

They came to a stop in front of Eugenie, seated on the ground, her father cradled in her lap.

"Have you no mercy? No humanity?" she cried. They did not respond.

"Shame on you. Shame on you all. This is not revolution. This is massacre. This is murder."

The face of the man at the front changed from expressionless to one full of hate. His eyes burned, his mouth turned down, and he bared his teeth. He swung his ax high, shouting, "Death to aristocrats!"

And as his ax swung down, Eugenie knew she would be the next victim of the revolution.

She awoke, screaming and suffocating, terrified in the darkness before her tumbling thoughts righted, and she remembered she was bound and gagged. Something bumped against her foot, and she screamed again into her disgusting gag, only to recall the second person in the coach. Reaching her foot out, she found the comforting ankle of the other coach dweller. Even though she could not see or hear that person, the comfort of another's presence was enough.

The carriage bumped to a stop, and Eugenie's heart rate soared. What was happening?

With a sway and a bump, the other woman was beside her again. She tried to cringe away, only to be met by a laugh.

"It's not as if you can go anywhere," the other woman said matter-of-factly. "Now, I come down here to tell you to stop that screaming. Only Ben and me can hear it, and it's doing nobody no good at all, you hear?"

Eugenie nodded her compliance but heard a muffled shouting from the other prisoner. She couldn't make out the words, but it was a youthful man's voice, and he seemed angry. She felt the young woman shift to the seat across from her.

"What's that, Jack?" she said sweetly. "Cat got your tongue?"

He tried to speak again, and the woman sighed heavily. "Oh, Jack, you can be so dull sometimes. I think it's time to be rid of you, my brother." Eugenie heard the click of the door and felt the cool air from outside, then to her horror, she heard Jack yelp before there was a thump, then silence.

The woman swung back up to the driver's seat and said, "Let's go home, Ben." She sounded dispirited like Eugenie herself was feeling. The coach felt much more empty and cold without her companion, no matter that she didn't know who he was or why he was there, and she prayed for his safety.

But soon, her hopes and prayers turned inward, and as the hours rolled on, she wondered if she would ever see her family again, or de Lacey, or even the sun. Tears dampened her blindfold. And her heart, which had not returned to a normal rhythm since she had been captured, battered the inside of her chest with its insistent thumping.

CHAPTER TWENTY-FOUR

De Lacey and Tatillion waited in the gathering gloom of the cool evening beneath a copse of trees that hid them from coaches and carts coming around the corner on the London Road. On the other side, two other hired men waited with them. Their dark, coarse clothing helped them to blend into the bushes ensuring that even after they had passed, coach drivers and passengers had no idea they were watched.

De Lacey shivered. This evening, they planned to pull the biggest heist ever, and he was concerned. They had not used additional men before, but the fact that the coach would most likely be carrying two or three beaters, as well as the coachman, necessitated it. Security on these larger deliveries had been tightened considerably since the highwaymen had started targeting the Waldershare Gang.

Tatillion gave a short whistle. He would be able to hear the approach of a large wagon much before de Lacey's ears would pick it up. Sure enough, a few moments later, de Lacey heard the hoof beats of a team of four approaching. At this time of the evening, at this particular spot on the road, it could only be the delivery coach.

De Lacey steadied his horse, all nerves taut. The horse must have sensed his anxiety, because it shuffled uncomfortably beneath him, blowing out a frustrated breath.

He waited for the coach to get within range, before shouting "Yah!" and urging his horse forward, Tatillion right behind him.

"Stand and deliver!" His pistol shot rang out, as did Tatillion's. The coach horses plunged and whinnied with fear, before coming to a stop. The driver glared at the two horsemen.

Without warning, six men poured out of the coach armed with pistols. They took aim at de Lacey and Tatillion at the same moment that de Lacey realized his hired thugs were nowhere to be seen. His heart skipped several beats. Tatillion cursed behind him apparently in realization of the double-cross.

De Lacey echoed Tatillion's curse when Arthur lumbered from the coach, his face far too calm for a man who had just been held up by brigands.

"Get them down." Arthur's short, sharp order was carried out with ruthless efficiency by the men, who approached en masse. De Lacey had no intention of killing anyone, and it seemed Arthur and his men knew it. They pulled de Lacey and Tatillion from their horses and tore away their pistols and their masks.

Arthur sauntered up to de Lacey, squinting in the gloom until his expression changed in recognition of de Lacey.

"Well. Jean."

To de Lacey Arthur didn't seem terribly surprised at discovering his identity. This, then, was the moment he had been waiting for.

"I told you I wanted out, Arthur." De Lacey looked the man square in the eye. "I'm happy to discontinue my disruption of your trade if you just leave me be."

"You're hardly in a position to be negotiating, lad." There was something chilling in the way Arthur's tone didn't change.

"Of course I am." De Lacey didn't allow the fear he felt to show in his voice. "I have something you want, and you have something I want."

"Do you really think it's that simple?"

In the shadowed evening, Arthur's face took on a sharper, angry look. "You've interrupted our supply lines to the point where some businesses don't want to trade with us anymore. You've upset the livelihoods of dozens of families. There are calls for you to be strung up."

From behind, de Lacey heard one of the men say under his breath, "Too right."

In an instant, de Lacey was afraid. This was not the response he had been expecting. Surely Arthur would not consider murdering him in cold blood.

"That's a little extreme, don't you think?"

Arthur nodded in agreement. "Yes, I do. I'm not interested in hanging anybody." Then he leered in de Lacey's face. "Much easier to shoot you, right here." De Lacey heard a click and realized that Arthur had a gun trained on him. Tatillion spoke a soft, "No," and then a grunt and de Lacey expected he had been cuffed to quieten him.

He didn't know what to think. He was so sure that his plan would word—that he could persuade the smugglers to let him go if only he could get their attention. But it seemed he had gambled with his own and Tatillion's life as well, and now, with the smuggler's attention well and truly drawn, it was over. He would never again get to kiss Eugenie's sweet lips, never again sit with Quincey at Brooks's, never again have Tatillion chide him for messing up his hair or his shoes or his cravat.

"You would kill a man in cold blood?"

"I've done it before. They don't find the bodies that we leave in the bogs."

The words, so cold, sent a chill through de Lacey. Then, he straightened up, shoulders back, and stared into Arthur's eyes.

"You must do what you must do, of course. And I must do what I must." So, saying, he executed a roundhouse kick, expertly knocking the gun out of Arthur's hand. The older man grunted in pain. De Lacey threw a quick follow up jab, which landed directly on Arthur's cheekbone and split the skin. A trickle of blood played down the man's face, as he lashed back out at de Lacey, landing a punch to his shoulder. Arthur was strong, as if from years of labor, and the blow hurt. De Lacey staggered back, but Arthur barrelled into him, pushing him to the ground and pummelling his face with blow after punishing blow. De Lacey struggled in the mud, his fists frustratingly blocked by Arthur's brutish and effective fighting style.

Then, in a moment of triumph, he got a hit off to Arthur's shoulder which made the man roar in pain and fury. He managed to pull himself out from under Arthur, staggering to his feet, fists raised, but Arthur's men restrained him. He was weakened from the fight but continued to struggle.

Arthur staggered up to him. Then, he drew back his fist and punched de Lacey in the stomach. De Lacey groaned and sagged in his captor's arms, but Arthur wasn't done. Again and again his fists connected with de Lacey's torso, until de Lacey was choking up blood.

Then, he heard the click of a pistol right by his ear.

Arthur wiped the blood from his cheek, his eyes hard. "Pull the trigger."

Before the man could do so, a sprightly sprung carriage crested the bend and slowed. The man quickly removed the gun from de Laceys' temple; however, he did not uncock it. To de Lacey's surprise, the yellow-wheeled carriage stopped, and his mouth dropped open as he recognised the seal on the door. The carriage opened, and Lord Edenburgh stepped down, his own pistol in hand, pointed directly at Arthur.

"Don't do it, Arthur," he commanded, "or I will shoot."

A tense standoff occurred for a moment as everyone attempted to work out exactly who held the upper hand. Then Arthur snapped, "Put down your weapons, lads."

De Lacey breathed a sigh of relief as he heard a dozen guns uncock. His captors let his arms go, and he nearly fell. He turned to his old friend, a stunned look on his face. "Arthur? You know each other?"

A smug smile was all the answer he got from Quincey, before the earl said to Arthur, "Shall we step aside my good fellow?" He put an arm around the older man and drew him to the side of the road, out of the hearing of the rest of the group.

De Lacey stood, bleeding and dumbfounded, as his society friend and his would-be murderer huddled. He heard Tatillion say, "Are you alright, monsieur?" But he couldn't say a word.

The two men walked back, and without a glance at de Lacey, Arthur said, "Alright you lot. Back in the coach." There was a murmur of discontent from the men, at once quelled by a frown from Arthur, and a harsh, "In the coach. Now."

The men sullenly got back in the coach, the driver whipped up the horses, and the vehicle sailed off into the night.

De Lacey numbly watched it go. The earl strolled up and stood beside him until the vehicle was gone. Then he said, "Shall we?" He turned to the manservant, who was watching the coach, from the other side of the road. "Tatillion, you're welcome to join us in the carriage."

He hopped into the coach, then turned to look at the two dumbfounded men. "Hurry up, gentlemen. We haven't got all night."

De Lacey stepped into the vehicle, feeling himself at odds with the opulent furnishings, his shabby clothes dark against the mustard velvet of the seats. He felt compelled to remove his tricorne, as did Tatillion.

De Lacey tried to breathe normally, fingering his ribs. Three, probably four of them were bruised or broken. The hand he had injured only weeks ago throbbed like the very devil. He suspected it was damaged again. Quite apart from that, he knew his face was covered in bruises and splits, and the inside of his mouth was slimy with blood. He pulled down the window and spat a gob out, then cursed as his chest and ribs screamed their displeasure.

Moving his shoulders tentatively, he glanced over at Lord Edenburgh. He was a magistrate. Just how would he react, knowing that his friend was a highwayman? There were stiff penalties for highway robbery—death and transportation among them. Would Quincey send him away to the colonies?

But the earl simply sat across from them, an inscrutable expression on his face, until de Lacey couldn't stand it anymore.

"How in blazes did you know to come out there?" he exploded. "What the devil are you about, Quincey?"

Lord Edenburgh smiled smugly. "My brandy supplies of late have been quite irregular. I receive some benefit, you know, from being the magistrate of the area and turning a blind eye."

"Benefit?" De Lacey was dumbfounded.

"Yes. Arthur and I have had a gentleman's agreement for quite a while. You, my friend, disturbed a perfectly acceptable arrangement, so I was forced into action."

De Lacey shook his head. "A gentleman's arrangement? Did you know I was with the gang?"

"Of course," scoffed Lord Edenburgh. "I've known since you stepped off the boat at Folkestone, nearly three years ago."

"So, the invitation to the card party?"

"A ruse, to be sure the highwayman was you. Arthur had already set up this fake coach delivery, to trap the highwaymen. When he told me of it, I knew I had to act, if you were to be saved."

"Then I owe you my life." De Lacey bowed as well as he could in the cramped confines of the carriage. "That, *mon ami*, is a debt I can never repay."

"You can repay me by resting from your nefarious ways."

"Indeed, I wish to. However, Arthur and his gang have been unwilling to sever the connection."

"Well, you need not bother about that anymore. Arthur has agreed to cut you loose."

"Really?" De Lacey looked up, hope in his eyes.

"Yes. For goodness sake, my good fellow, I don't wish to be out and about saving you more than this once. As it is, I'm missing a magnificent party at Mrs. Wilberforce's estate. She might be a sour-faced old codfish, and her daughter as ugly as a toad, but she does provide some excellent champagne for her guests."

The grin on Lord Edenburgh's face showed he was not unhappy. And as for de Lacey, he was delighted. He was free of the smugglers. Free! He felt giddy and heard himself laugh out loud. He grabbed Lord Edenburgh's hand in a crushing grip between his own two hands. "*Mon ami*, you have made me the happiest man alive."

"Oh no," protested his lordship. "That will never do. Those are the words you need to speak to Mademoiselle Ponnette, just as soon as she accepts your proposal. Which, I assume, you will go and do first thing tomorrow morning?"

"Indeed, I will," replied de Lacey with a broad smile.

CHAPTER TWENTY-FIVE

"What do we do now?" asked Ben—the man who had assisted the young woman in Eugenie's capture.

"We wait." There was a smugness to the girl's tone that confused Eugenie. Wait?

Before she could ask the question, Ben said, "For what?"

"For de Lacey, of course."

Eugenie was battered, filthy and confused. The barn beside The Ancient Crow Inn was quiet and tidy, and it was there the young woman had taken her. She didn't know where The Ancient Crow Inn was, except that it seemed they passed by a village before they reached it—she had heard the sounds of small industry and commerce as they drove along. Her hopes for rescue seemed to be diminishing since nobody would even know where she was.

Ben looked confused. "Jean? He won't come here. He's not due for another meeting until the week after next when the Karenina docks."

"Oh, he'll be here. And when he arrives, we'll see just who it is that he loves."

The words were almost spat at Eugenie. At that moment, she realized just what was going on. Cold fury started to build in her. She was here, scared and bruised and dirty because de Lacey couldn't keep his hands off another woman. De Lacey, who insisted that he loved her. Hah! He could no more love one single woman than a fish could breathe outside of the water.

A quiet sob escaped her lips, enough to draw the attention of the young woman.

"Quit your crying," she said. "There'll be plenty to cry about later, when your intended gets here."

"My intended? I don't know what you mean."

The girl stood and pointed the gun at Eugenie. "Don't play coy with me, lady. I know you've been chasing Jean all over London. Well, he's mine, do you hear? Mine. I bagged him as soon as he got off the boat from Calais."

"I'm not sure what Monsieur de Lacey said to you…"

"He said he loved me. He said he wanted to be with me."

"But he would never marry you. You must see that." Eugenie tried a quiet and reasonable tone, but it was of no use.

"Shut up," the girl screamed. "He will marry me. I will be his Lady."

It was this moment that Ben chose to interrupt, his boorish features confused. "I thought you loved me, Maggie. I thought you said you'd be with me when all this was done."

Eugenie felt a little sorry for the stupid, love struck, and obviously duped Ben. "She used you, Ben," she said kindly. "She never meant to be with you."

"No!" Ben charged at Eugenie and slapped her hard across the mouth. Her head jerked around, and she felt a trickle of blood from the corner of her lip. "She loves me. She always has. You're nothing but a stuck-up foreign bitch who thinks she's better than all of us."

"You tell her, Ben," replied Maggie loftily, waving the pistol about. "Of course, I love you."

"See?"

Eugenie sighed. The simple-minded Ben would not be her salvation. "What makes you think de Lacey will come? He has not declared for me. It is just as likely that my family will send trackers, or that the local magistrate will attend."

"No, he will be here. My brother will tell him. And Jean would not risk your reputation." This, she said in a sing-song voice. "He will alert as few people as possible, and come here himself to rescue you. But he will take one look at me, and remember where

147

his heart lies."

The girl was mad. Mad with an obvious unrequited passion for de Lacey. She cursed him under her breath.

"Come along, Ben. We need to get this girl into the last stall. Then…" Maggie trailed a finger down Ben's arm, suggesting bounty that he couldn't help but be interested in. Eugenie was yanked to her feet and would have fallen if not for Ben's meaty hand around her upper arm. She stumbled into the last stall, pushed by the too-eager brute.

She thought perhaps she could kick at the door of the stall with her feet, only to her dismay, she was seated on what seemed to be a milking stool. Not only were her arms tied and her filthy gag pulled back up, but Maggie instructed that her feet be tied to the stool as well. Then, Maggie and Ben left her there, alone, in the dark of the last stall. She could hear Maggie's seductive tones beguiling the poor, stupid Ben as they left.

She felt bereft. Where, oh where, were her rescuers? They would have discovered her abduction hours ago. She thought it must be close to midnight—while she couldn't see much, the moonlight had streamed into the barn when her blindfold was removed. Surely there would have been people sent out as soon as Rachel had arrived home and sounded the alarm. Surely there would be rescuers on their way.

Surely de Lacey would be coming to rescue her. *Non*?

A moment later, she lifted her chin and straightened her back.

No, Eugenie, nobody is coming for you. You must rescue yourself. It has been done before. You can do it again.

The horse in the stable next to her whickered, and she was somehow comforted to know there was another beast with her there in the dark. Under her revolting gag, she grimaced.

What did she need to do first?

CHAPTER TWENTY-SIX

The tired horses clopped into Jermyn Street. It was late, most of the evening's festivities had already ceased. The street lighting did little to pierce the foggy gloom.

De Lacey and Tatillion waited for the coach to stop, then Tatillion helped the injured de Lacey exit the coach. Every step was insufferable, and de Lacey wasn't sure he would even make it to his door.

"Tatillion? Get someone to come and have a look at those ribs, won't you? And his hand." Lord Edenburgh had been quiet during the drive home, but every time de Lacey had opened his weary eyes, he had seen his friend's sharp eyes upon him. Quincey was concerned.

As well he might be, however, de Lacey realized he probably looked a lot worse than he felt. His injured ribs made it difficult to breathe, and his hand felt like it was palpably pulsating along with his heartbeat, but all in all, considering the beating he had received, he was in relatively good shape.

Tatillion shut the door, and the coach moved on, swallowed up by the night.

The weariness ate into his bones, making it difficult to lift one foot up after another, even if it was only to cross the street to reach his lodgings.

But before he could reach the doorstep, a figure jumped up from the step. De Lacey and Tatillion tensed for a moment before de Lacey waved Tatillion down. It was Jack.

Tatillion let go of de Lacey to pull out his pistol and cock it in the young man's face. De Lacey stumbled but kept himself upright. He was suspicious. Jack was one of the smugglers.

"What do you want, Jack?"

"It's Maggie, Jean." The youngster didn't take his eyes off the pistol pointed at his chest.

"She's not my concern. Tatillion."

Tatillion held the pistol in place for another second and then uncocked it with a scowl. He returned to de Lacey's side to assist him.

Jack's eyes boggled. "What happened to you?" When he received no reply, he leaped to stand in front of de Lacey's door.

De Lacey sighed. "Jack, just go away, will you? Haven't the Waldershare Gang done enough for tonight?"

He tried to push past the young man, but Jack held his ground.

"Maggie has kidnapped your lady."

"What lady?"

"Your Mademoiselle Ponnette."

"What?" De Lacey was instantly awake. "Come inside and explain yourself, Jack."

"There's no time, Jean. I don't know what she's capable of." The whine in Jack's voice reminded de Lacey of his own impetuous youth.

"There is time," he said, surprising himself. "Tatillion is going to have to patch me up before we can do anything. Come inside, have some brandy, tell me everything."

Tatillion, held open the front door, so the three men walked the corridor quietly to de Lacey's rooms. Jack wanted to chatter immediately, but de Lacey shushed him, thinking of all the other men asleep in the other rooms. The walls were thin, and until they were inside de Lacey's chambers, they needed to stay quiet.

Tatillion bowed de Lacey in, and Jack followed him. De Lacey had never received him into his rooms before, and the young man whistled appreciatively. "Nice house."

De Lacey, surprised, looked around. To him, the rooms were cramped and dark, with little to recommend them except their price and their proximity to the center of London's social districts. But he could see how a young man from the country, whose whole family were thrust into a tiny, shingled house, would be impressed.

"Tatillion, brandy if you please, for all of us—and water and bandages."

Tatillion hurried to the decanter while de Lacey continued. "Now Jack. Tell me what this is all about." Waving Jack into an easy chair, he noticed red marks on Jack's wrists. "Is Maggie in trouble? Are you?"

"I think she's gone mad, Jean."

"Mad?"

"Yes. She convinced herself that you were going to marry her. When you said you wouldn't, that day at the inn, well, she's just become queerer and queerer since." Jack regarded him reproachfully. "She was an innocent before you met her you know, Jean."

De Lacey raised an eyebrow. He could advise Jack otherwise, but he thought the correct response, for now, was silence.

"She swanned around the house, insisting on doing no work because she would soon be a lady. Mama boxed her ears more than once, but she wouldn't be dissuaded." Jack was visibly disgusted with his sister.

De Lacey frowned, absently accepting a glass from Tatillion. "But I told her we could never…"

"She was sure there would be a way."

De Lacey sighed and shook his head. "What happened then?"

"She got more and more angry, you know, at you, but more at the mademoiselle, shouting that she didn't deserve you, that she was the only one who loved you, that you had said you loved her and all those other sickly things women say." Jack took a gulp of the brandy Tatillion had pressed into his hand. "I say, this is magnificent brandy. Much better than the whiskey we get at home."

"Pigswill," muttered Tatillion, but de Lacey held up his hand to silence him.

"Back to the story Jack."

Jack nodded, finishing off the brandy with a second gulp. "Early this morning she stole old man Greaves' coach and charmed Ben into driving it—you know Ben, he's been sick in love with Maggie for years—and they drove to London to find her. Old man Greaves came to our place shouting and swearing for Papa to pay for the damage to his barn and for the hire of the coach."

De Lacey didn't care about old man Greaves. "What happened, Jack?" He said through gritted teeth.

"They drove up here and took mademoiselle while she was walking, with her maid screaming at them and half of London watching."

"Excuse me," interrupted Tatillion very politely, but with a hint of iron in his voice. De Lacey, surprised at his servant's interjection, turned to him and said, "What is it Tatillion?"

"I wonder how the young gentleman knows all this?"

Jack flushed. "I wasn't in on it," he said defensively, throwing a scowl at Tatillion. "When I heard they'd gone I hopped on the farm horse and got to London as quick as I could. Poor old Brutus. It took us hours and hours. I tracked Maggie down—she doesn't really know London very well, there were only a couple of places she might be—and tried to reason with her. She had Ben punch my lights out." Jack flushed again. "When I came to, I was inside the coach, trussed up like a Christmas swine. Then I heard your mademoiselle get in, and Maggie tie her up and blindfold her. I tried to comfort her, but the only thing I could do was rest my foot against hers. And about an hour out of London, they opened up the coach and threw me out on the road."

De Lacey nodded to Tatillion to give Jack more brandy. It sounded as if the lad deserved it.

"Anyways, so I sat there for a few minutes in the mud, wondering what I should do." Now, Jack seemed disgusted at himself. "I was well nigh useless, with no idea how I would get out of my restraints when a man comes up and removes the ties around my wrist. They'd seen me pitched from the coach, you see, and didn't dare to approach for a little while. I thanked them heartily, then ran back into town, to find you. Only you weren't at your rooms."

De Lacey nodded and finished the rest of his brandy. "Come," he said decisively, standing up. "We have no time to waste."

Jack and Tatillion looked at him uncertainly.

"Both of you, now!"

They jumped up, and de Lacey rushed them back outside and into an early morning hack, and straight over to Underwood House.

His strident knock on the door was answered within moments by a butler who had obviously been awake for a good portion of the night. While he was everything that was proper, his eyes were red rimmed, and his skin pale.

"I've come to see Madame Ponnette," de Lacey said, pushing the astonished butler aside and ushering his two companions in with him. "I am de Lacey."

"Yes, sir, I know who you are, but madame is abed." The butler's deep disapproval of this early morning bombardment was evident in his tone.

"Come now, do you think she has slept at all this evening? Tell her that I am here."

De Lacey's tone broached no argument, so the butler bowed and had the message sent to Madame Ponnette, then he ushered the three men into a downstairs room.

Shortly thereafter Madame Ponnette rushed into the room, night attire covered by a robe and her yellow curls adrift under a cap. She, too, looked pale, with blue eyes made enormous by the dark circles around them.

"Monsieur de Lacey, do you have news?" She said, grasping his arm desperately.

Before he could answer, both Lord and Lady Underwood came into the room as well, having been disturbed from their sleep by their respective servants.

"What is the meaning of this?" Lord Underwood demanded. "What kind of a gentleman calls at this hour?"

"Oh, hush, Hugh." Madame Ponnette's reprimand obviously

surprised Lord Underwood for he fell silent. De Lacey wanted to cheer for the little French woman, but instead, he told her the story Jack had told him.

"And so, you see, I know where she is, and who has her. I don't expect Maggie will harm her—even in her altered state I don't think Maggie would have it in her to do that—but I must go to Waldershare immediately. However, I didn't want to go without letting you know that she will be found."

Madame Ponnette looked as if she wanted to hug him, but her step toward him was interrupted by a loud harrumph from Lord Underwood, who advanced instead, a cold expression on his face.

"So, correct me if I am wrong, but without your interest in Mademoiselle Ponnette in the first place, none of this would have happened?"

De Lacey hung his head. "No, my Lord, I don't believe it would have. I take full responsibility for Mademoiselle Ponnette's current predicament."

"As well you might, young man. You seem more the villain of this piece than the hero." Madame Ponnette squeaked in outraged disagreement.

"*Non*, Hugh, but he is to go and rescue Eugenie. His motives have always been pure. Have they not, vicomte?"

De Lacey nodded and tried not to smile as he realized it was the first time in his life he could truly admit to pure motives.

But Lord Underwood seemed to notice his near smirk, and reprimanded, "And exactly what interest do you have in Mademoiselle Ponnette, monsieur?" he asked. When Madame Ponnette protested again, he waved her off. "No, Anselle, this time I need an answer."

There was a short silence before de Lacey straightened his back, looked Lord Underwood in the eye, and said, "I wish to marry her."

"Is that so? And exactly what recommends you for marriage to her?"

De Lacey took a breath and smiled wryly. "I have no money or property at the moment if that is what you are asking. Emigrating has left me destitute until my lands are returned to me. But I offer Mademoiselle Ponnette my heart and soul. I love her." His smile widened. "With a grand passion."

Madame Ponnette elbowed her way past her brother-in-law and took de Lacey's hands. "Then that is enough for me." She lifted herself up on her tiptoes and kissed him on the cheek. "Go, *mon cher*. Go save your love. And bring her back home to me."

"I will."

CHAPTER TWENTY-SEVEN

It didn't seem to matter that de Lacey was exhausted, or that he had found a moderately comfortable position in the swaying carriage, his injuries and anxiety kept him from sleep. Across from him, Tatillion snored gently, his head resting on Jack's shoulder. Jack too had succumbed to the lure of sleep. However, de Lacey wondered if he should wake the lad—his head lolled alarmingly with each bump of the carriage. He decided to allow Jack the luxury of sleep, even if he himself couldn't indulge.

Every time he thought he might drift off, his thoughts flicked to Eugenie: where she might be, how she was being treated, whether she was hurt. Had Maggie hurt her? How would he respond if Maggie had done so?

He simply couldn't rest knowing the woman he wanted to marry and cherish—dammit, the woman he loved—was in danger.

He loved her. The sensation was at once heady and frightening. It was nothing he had ever experienced before. And he had hardly touched her! He wanted to. He ached to run his fingers along the curve of her hip and down her milky thigh, to kiss her in a thousand places, to make sweet love to her in front of a roaring fire.

To know that he would happily give his life for her, that he would happily kill for her, well, it was overwhelming.

De Lacey himself was surprised by the heat of his anger toward Maggie. His cultivated mask of quiet cynicism had its beginnings in his even temper and sense of the ridiculous. But right now, were Maggie in front of him, he truly believed he would take her by the throat and choke the life out of her. Ten hours in the coach had his teeth on edge and his fists permanently clenched. Still, he kept his feelings in check, even as Eugenie was treated with God knows what discourtesy by a foolish maiden with grand pretensions. It made him unwell to dwell on it.

Maggie's life experience didn't extend much past the borders of her small village, so he didn't expect she had concocted any grandiose schemes for Eugenie's kidnapping. She had probably ensconced Eugenie somewhere, awaiting de Lacey's appearance. Well, he certainly would appear, and make it very clear that she would suffer for her wickedness.

He knew it was pointless, and probably detrimental to his composure. However, he turned over and over in his mind the filthy places Maggie might have thought to hide Eugenie. It would be somewhere quite obvious. Maggie wished de Lacey to find her so she could have her twisted moment of triumph. In his mind, he fiercely promised that she would get that moment. Only, perhaps not the moment she expected.

De Lacey had watched the glistening orb of the sun rise as their journey began. He had watched it arc overhead, flittering like a skittish maiden in and out of the clouds as they raced south east. And it was lower, and turning a deep, fiery orange in the sky when they finally arrived at their destination, The Ancient Crow Inn.

Stepping out of the carriage, de Lacey steadied himself against the side as his legs buckled underneath him and he nearly stumbled. Lightheaded and with a roiling stomach, he swallowed the bile that threatened to rise. He needed to get this business over with, take Eugenie back to London, and then sleep for two days straight.

Entering the inn, his senses were assailed by the stink of stale beer, urine, and perspiration. Tankards stood, half empty, on tables, which were slick with spills. De Lacey had never seen the inn in such neglect.

"Jean! Thank the Lord you're here!" Mistress Finchley threw herself into his arms. "My Maggie is gone! And Jack too!"

Despite Mistress Finchley's warm welcome, de Lacey stiffened as he glanced at the stony faces of the men in the room—the very men who had the day before, planned his murder. Suspicion radiated off them. De Lacey felt Tatillion's presence at his shoulder, and a quick glance his way revealed his faithful servant had his weapon at the ready.

"What are you doing here?" Thomas Finchley's voice was ice. "We didn't expect to see you again."

"I didn't expect to be here," de Lacey replied dryly. "However, your children are creating issues that I have no choice but to attend."

De Lacey pulled Jack through the door. His mother abandoned de Lacey to hug her son in a fierce embrace. "Where were you, Jack? Are you all right? Never disappear like that again." She pushed the hair off his face, and kissed him. Jack accepted her caresses with poor grace, only saying, "I had to mum. Maggie took herself to London. She's in trouble."

"What kind of trouble?" Thomas shot a dark look at de Lacey who threw up his hands.

"It's nothing I've done. It's all her own doing. And I'm going to throttle the wench when I find her."

Mistress Finchley's shoulders slumped as she groaned. "She confronted your lady, didn't she? The stupid girl. I told her to quit thinking she could rise above her station, but that girl has never listened." While she spoke, Mistress Finchley took in de Lacey's injuries, wincing as she touched his bruised face.

But while her words were directed at de Lacey, Jack answered her. "She didn't just confront her, mum. She kidnapped her."

Mistress Finchley's hand flew to cover her heart and she stumbled back, only her husband's kindly grasp prevented her from falling. De Lacey's sharp eyes took in the sudden discomfort of the men, choosing that moment to ask for their help.

"I need your assistance, monsieurs, this one last time. There is a young lady out there—cold and alone and probably terrified. I beg of you, help me to find her."

A murmur of agreement rippled through the men before Mistress Finchley responded plaintively, "But Jean? She didn't come home last night."

De Lacey swore. He was sure she would have come back to the inn—if she hadn't come home, finding Eugenie would be even more difficult. "In that case, we need to search the entire village."

"That girl has no shame," her father muttered. Mistress Finchley turned on him, a look of fury on her face, but he shrugged. "It's true. She's always been a wild 'un."

"But not wicked, Mr. Finchley. Never wicked." Mistress Finchley's look of entreaty encompassed not only her husband but all the people in the room.

De Lacey was unmoved. "She's kidnapped an innocent young woman. That's wicked enough for me."

Jack piped up. "And she had Ben knock me out, and she tied me up and threw me out of a coach."

The innkeeper looked confused. "I think we'd better have the whole story from you, lad."

De Lacey shook his head. "What we need to do is start searching for Mademoiselle Ponnette. Each moment she is here, she will be more distressed, and possibly in even more danger."

The innkeeper took his wife in his arms as she dissolved into new, fitful tears. "I'll gather the boys back here, and we'll search proper like for this mademoiselle of yours." He regarded de Lacey coldly, and the ice returned to his tone. "But once she's found, I never want to see your face around here again, Jean de Lacey. I don't care how fine a gentleman you are in France. Here, you've destroyed my daughter's happiness, ruined her mind, and damaged my family."

It hurt de Lacey's heart to hear a man he still thought of as a friend denounce him so roundly, but he knew the words were true. Without him, Maggie would still be merrily carousing with the boys of the village, Eugenie would not be in the terrible fix she was in, and Maggie's family would not be in ruins.

He nodded sadly, blinking back his tears. "In that case, we had better get started."

Before they could move, a man rushed through the inn door. "We found her!"

Both de Lacey and Mistress Finchley rounded on the man. "Who?" they both demanded together.

He looked confused. "Maggie, of course."

"Where is she?"

"She's on the village green. But Mistress?" The man hesitated for a moment before he blurted out, "She's drunk as a lord, and Ben Trenchard is with her."

His jaw set and his eyes flashing, de Lacey stormed out of the inn and down the gravel road to the green, followed closely by Tatillion, the Finchleys, and all the other folk.

They had heard Maggie before they saw her. She and Ben were bellowing out a bawdy tune:

"Now I think I will make me best way home
If me mother ask me why I've been so long,
I'll say I've been ground by a score or more
But I've never been ground so well before."

Maggie's mother flushed. "She's singing about having her corn ground by the miller," she explained earnestly, but her husband stopped her with a wave of his hand and a slow shake of his head.

"Hush, love, we all know what she's singing about."

The group was silent as they approached the pair, seated on the green. Maggie held a tankard in her hand, hair and dress askew. She didn't even register her father's presence until he strode up to her and toed her with his boot. "So, Maggie, this is what you make of yourself?"

"Papa!" She scrambled to her feet guiltily, dropping the tankard. She swayed, and her father gripped her arm to keep her from falling. She then sent up a caterwauling that stretched de Lacey's nerves even further.

"Stop it, Papa, you're hurting me."

It seemed her noise grated on her father's nerves as well. "It won't be the worst hurt I inflict on you today, you no-good besom," he muttered. He turned back, taking Maggie with him. It was only then that she spied de Lacey.

"Jean!" She ran toward him and threw herself into his arms. His already delicate stomach churned at the liquor fumes about her, but he had to know where Eugenie was. So, instead of flinging her away, he disengaged himself with care, and placed his hands on her shoulders, looking into her unfocused eyes.

"Where is Mademoiselle Ponnette, Maggie?" he asked in a tone that brooked no opposition.

Maggie pouted. "Oh, her." She stared into de Lacey's eyes and licked her lips seductively. De Lacey tried not to shudder in revulsion as she ran a finger along his arm. "You know I can love you better than she can."

"Maggie!" her mother and Ben gasped at the same time. She spun around to face the two of them, somewhat staggering in the process.

"Well, it's true." A self-satisfied smile crossed her face. "Ben'll tell you." She giggled, returning her attention to de Lacey, while her mother glared at Ben, and the townspeople shuffled uncomfortably. "What do you say?"

Jack came to stand beside de Lacey and eyed his sister with undisguised disgust. "You're a disgrace to this family, and to yourself."

"You," she spat. "You can't tell me what to do. I'm going to be a lady." She smiled upon de Lacey again. "Jean loves me. He said so."

"You know he didn't, you draggle-tail."

"He did." She pouted, and angry tears fell from her eyes. "When we patched him up after he was laid into, he said he loved me. You heard him."

"He was delirious with pain."

"He still said it."

Jack shook his head, frustrated with the conversation. "Even if he did, he didn't mean it."

"He did so!" By now, Maggie was shouting, her voice holding

an edge of insanity. "He loves me, and only me. Tell them, Jean."

"Maybe if you tell me where Mademoiselle Ponnette is first, then we'll talk."

"Tell them, Jean." Her voice became more insistent and shrill.

"I won't do it, Maggie. I don't love you."

"You do! You do!"

With each foolish word out of her mouth, de Lacey became more and more impatient with Maggie and was readying himself to shake the girl, to slap her, to do whatever was necessary to get the information from her, when she said, "One kiss, Jean. Just give me one kiss."

He colored, and looked over at her parents. Mistress Finchley was still sobbing into her hands, but Thomas glared at him. It couldn't be helped. If it would take kissing Maggie to bring Eugenie to safety, he would do it.

He stepped in closer to her, repulsed by the look and smell of her, but grasped her around the shoulders and planted a firm kiss on her lips.

She responded by throwing her arms around his head and holding him, pinned, in the kiss. He very nearly gagged, surprised and shocked that a woman he was happy to lay with just a few short weeks ago could be so disgusting to him now.

"Ha!" she said, finally letting him go. "You see? You can't kiss me like that and say you don't love me." De Lacey pursed his lips, unwilling to say anything.

Taking his silence as proof of de Lacey's devotion in her own deranged mind, she said, "Come on. I'll show you where the girl is."

CHAPTER TWENTY-EIGHT

Maggie turned and with her unsteady gait, made her way back to the inn, continuing to belt out the ditty, and at one stage, she started to dance, until she caught sight of de Lacey's face, and returned to demure walking. De Lacey wondered if he should feel pity for her parents, who trudged meekly along behind, clearly mortified by their daughter's behavior. These were good, hard-working folk who didn't deserve this public humiliation. Still, reflected de Lacey, if they had better control over their daughter, she wouldn't now be leading them all on a merry dance. De Lacey swore his own daughters, should he ever have any, would be well schooled in how unattractive debauchery was.

When they reached the inn, Maggie took them around the back and into the gloomy stables. She pointed at the far stall.

As de Lacey's eyes grew accustomed to the dusky light, he peered into the stall, both eager and afraid of what he might find.

But the stall was empty.

"She's not here," he shouted, striding back to Maggie and grabbing her by the shoulders. Shaking her, he said, "Where is she, Maggie? Where is she?"

Maggie looked confused, and then furious. "I don't know."

"There!" Jack shouted, and de Lacey turned to where he was pointing. Out in the field, a figure was hurrying away, rapidly getting smaller.

"Eugenie!" he called, but she was too far away to hear. He pulled away from Maggie and started bolting across the field; his eyes fixed on his prize, heedless of the protestations of his ribs.

He closed the distance between them, quickly at first, but becoming slower and slower as his battered body refused to go on. Falling to his knees, he shouted "Eugenie!" with all the force he could muster.

She hesitated and turned around.

"De Lacey?"

She turned and started to run toward him.

Maggie shouted, "Stop!"

Maggie had arrived, along with everyone else who could run the distance—Jack and Tatillion and several of the men. The Finchleys struggled forward, slower than the rest.

From somewhere about her person, Maggie had pulled a pistol. She swaggered toward Eugenie and stood facing her, only a dozen feet between them. Eugenie's smile froze on her face, her eyes flicking to de Lacey.

"Now, Jean, tell her. Tell her you love me. That you're going to marry me." Maggie's voice was full of confidence. "If you don't, I'm going to shoot her in the head." De Lacey saw Eugenie's eyes widen. Her gaze fixed on the pistol.

De Lacey's insides churned with rage, worsening as he realized just how useless he was with Maggie holding the weapon.

"Maggie!" her father remonstrated. "You'll do no such thing." To de Lacey, it seemed as if Thomas' feet were frozen to the spot, his words a last-ditch effort to control his wayward daughter. They seemed to have the opposite effect.

"I will," she raged. "I'll shoot her." She cocked the pistol and aimed it at Eugenie, who took a more solid stance and glared at Maggie with disdain.

"Wait just a moment," de Lacey said soothingly, his hands in front of him in a conciliatory gesture. "Maggie, *chérie*, we can fix this. Give me the pistol. I promise nothing will happen to you." His voice, purposefully soft and soothing, seemed to evaporate Maggie's rage, and her harsh stance started to soften.

In that moment, the situation exploded.

Ben charged the group, in a drunken rage, a pistol in hand.

"You can't have Maggie. She's mine!" he roared. He aimed and took a shot at de Lacey, who only just managed to sidestep the bullet by desperately diving to the left.

In the same moment, Maggie turned in surprise toward Ben's loud voice, and her gun discharged.

There was a long, heart-stopping silence. The smoke from the two weapons drifted lazily into the darkening sky, though the tang of gunpowder hung, heavy and potent in the air.

Then Ben gasped. He took a step backward and dropped his weapon. He looked down as if puzzled by the perfectly round hole in his chest. The wound began to trickle with blood, and Ben looked up at Maggie in astonishment, dropped to his knees, and then to the side.

Maggie screamed as if she had been the one shot. She rushed toward Ben, falling to her knees and scooping his lifeless body into her arms. "No!" she screamed, and the animalistic wail sent a shudder up de Lacey's spine.

De Lacey spun toward Eugenie. She stared back at him as the color drained from her face and her eyes rolled back. Dashing toward her, he managed to catch her and support her as she fell. Frantically, he searched her body for a wound. He was unable to locate one.

"Is she hurt?" asked Jack.

"I can't find a wound." De Lacey stood, lifting his precious bundle in his arms. He stared down woodenly at Maggie, who was weeping over Ben's body. Thomas stepped forward and took the pistol from the slack hand of his daughter.

"I'm sorry, Ben. I didn't mean to shoot. I wasn't going to shoot anyone. Don't die, Ben. I didn't mean it. I just wanted Jean to… but I don't. I don't love him, Ben. I love you. Don't die, my love."

Her father pried her away from Ben's body and pulled her up into his arms. "Shush, love. Come inside." He wearily transferred his burden to his wife, who then led the still weeping girl toward the inn.

There was silence as de Lacey and Thomas Finchley glared at each other. Then the innkeeper said under his breath, "Do ye not think she's suffered enough?"

All of de Lacey's anger toward Maggie melted, and he was left with nothing but bone-weariness. He could not care less about Maggie's suffering. As far as he was concerned, she earned all the contempt and ridicule that would be heaped upon her. Right now, his one concern was to return the beautiful, unconscious woman in his arms to her mother, and to the care of a competent doctor. He caught Thomas' eye and saw a glimmer of gratitude. Then, without another word, he carried Eugenie to his coach, Tatillion trailing along behind.

CHAPTER TWENTY-NINE

When the bullet whizzed past her face, a thousand images exploded in Eugenie's mind. Images she had tried to escape. Images she had hoped she would never see again.

Her lady's maid, Liliana, lying facedown on the cold ground, a smoking bullet hole in her back.

She and her mother desperately escaping their Paris chateau, moments before it was overrun by a mob of maniacal revolutionaries.

And worst of all, her poor *papa*, his arms and stomach torn to ribbons as he ran through the axes and lances, murdered at Abbaye Prison.

They hadn't been dreams—they were memories. Her father was dead, cut down in his prime by a bloodthirsty mob of murderers.

She fell into a jumbled vortex of memories, the colors over bright and intense.

Her happy childhood, in the gardens at their chateaux in Paris, the scent of roses and honeysuckle pervading every corner of her secret hideaway. Blooms of every color burst forth with each step she took, underfoot a verdant spread of a thousand different greens. But the flowers started to ooze red and the grass withered under her feet, leaving only rocks and shale. Her feet were torn by the gravel, and she fell to her knees, crying.

Inside, her mother smiled at Eugenie as she descended the sweeping staircase. She met Eugenie's father at the door, he took her in his arms and tenderly kissed her cheek. Eugenie knew they were in love. She didn't exactly know how, but she knew.

But they were in danger. The windows dripped with blood, and the house was shrouded in darkness. Still, her parents stared into each other's eyes, oblivious to the changes all around them. Eugenie tried to scream, tried to warn them. But her voice was silent, and she was forced to watch as a wave of darkness engulfed them. It was only then that she could scream.

Traveling through Paris, she could see the signs of division— here, a man wrote a republican slogan on the side of a building, there, a woman shouted over the disparity between taxes on nobles and common people. Eugenie felt terrified of the hatred in the woman's gaze and voice, both directed at Eugenie, while the six small children grasping at the woman's skirts—all of them with enormous blank eyes and stick-like bodies—opened their mouths, and all manner of insects crawled out, covering the woman and her children in a seething, buzzing shroud.

Then, she found herself dancing at a society ball, clasped firm in the grasp of an unknown gentleman, the people gay and laughing. To her horror, the walls started to seep blood. It dribbled down the walls, pooling on the parquet flooring, and then spreading out until it reached the dancers' feet. They didn't even seem to notice they were dancing in it, even though the blood had climbed almost to their ankles. All the ladies' gowns had bright red rings around the bottom, but their brittle laughter and coquettish teasing never wavered. Eugenie wanted to shout at them, to tell them of the horror, to warn them, but she could not open her mouth. Her voice could not be heard. Tears sprung to her eyes.

She wrested herself from the slack grasp of her oblivious partner and ran out into the street. It was a bright day, still monochrome, and she stood at the far end of the square, across from the Abbaye Prison.

Eugenie swallowed down the bile from the metallic tang of blood all around. All she could see were the bodies of those slain by the murderers—and all she could feel was a numb acceptance of the fates of the prisoners. That is, until her own *papa* ran through the archway, a spot of bright color against the black and white of Paris.

Eugenie shrieked as he threw his arms up to protect his head. Swords and axes slashed at his body as he ran, and a cheer went up from the crowd. His arms, torso, and legs were shredded. But he managed to make it through the grisly arch before he collapsed.

She sobbed and ran to him, her grief giving her the strength to pull him away from the people and over to a sheltered corner. Her *papa* lay in her arms, breathing his last, his body unable to withstand the damage that had been thrust upon it. He lifted one bloodied hand to caress her cheek.

"My beautiful girl, you must be strong," he whispered. Blood seeped from the side of his mouth.

"I can't," sobbed Eugenie, holding him. "*Papa*, I don't know how."

"You are stronger than you know."

With that, his hand dropped and his beautiful eyes, exactly the color of Eugenie's, closed forever. Eugenie howled, loud and long. The people close by stop to laugh and spit upon them both, and Eugenie's grief and fear dissolved, replaced by such anger as she had never felt before. Her entire body shook. After laying her father's body down tenderly, she slowly rose to stand, her haughty, furious gaze on the people round about.

"Murderers!" she raged. "This is not revolution. This is massacre."

More people turned to her, their mouths agape.

"May God judge you to the fiery depths of hell."

A man stepped forward and pointed at her. His deep, sepulchral words would spell her doom.

"You are not a patriot."

Out of nowhere, Eugenie's mother appeared, weeping and pulling her away. "Eugenie, *chérie*, we must go now."

Eugenie couldn't tear her eyes from her father's corpse.

"You will be targeted, darling."

He lay, a peaceful smile on his face despite the wickedness all about. The roar of the crowds dulled.

"We must leave France."

Eugenie only smiled, knowing that up in heaven, her *papa* was at peace.

"Now, Eugenie!"

The shock of her mother's palm against her cheek brought the noise of the crowd and the dangerous situation back into focus.

She and her mother dashed home, breathlessly telling the servants what had happened, and offering them sanctuary if they came to England. Some spat at Eugenie as they left to join the revelers. Some bowed low, explaining they didn't wish Madame Ponnette or Eugenie any harm, they simply wished to be with their own families.

And some, Liliana, Rachel, and others, agreed to travel to England. Their eyes were fearful but resolute. Arrangements were made—so quickly that Eugenie thought there must have been provisions already in place for the contingency. Her mother handed her an underskirt, covered in pockets in which documents and jewels had been secreted. She told Eugenie to put it on under her dress. She was doing the same with another underskirt, as was Liliana.

Eugenie suddenly cried out. "Isabeau!" She knew it foolish, but she couldn't bear for her beautiful cat to be left behind. Isabeau would be dead in days.

"I already have her," replied faithful Rachel, swinging a hatbox from which a low growl proceeded. Eugenie smiled at her, relieved.

They crept out of the house via the kitchen entrance—a door Eugenie had never used before in her life. They ran to an open carriage that stood at the far gate; still, they were almost too late.

Gunshots rang out, and Eugenie felt someone shove her into the bushes. Dizzily righting herself, her eyes widened as there was Liliana, a pool of blood slowly seeping into the ground below her. More shots were fired, and Eugenie couldn't contain her shriek of fear. One of the groomsmen took a bullet graze across the thigh, but with assistance, he could hobble to the carriage.

And then, they were in the carriage, flying across the

cobblestones and away from life as they knew it, far away to distant relatives in a distant land.

CHAPTER THIRTY

De Lacey hadn't been permitted into the house when they had first arrived, Eugenie being stolen from his hands and dispatched into the house. But her mother had stayed for a moment to thank him, and to invite him back the following morning once he was cleaned up and rested. He had smiled—he must have looked like a raggedy corpse, still dressed in his highwayman outfit, and with two days of stubble and sleep deprivation on his face.

He didn't think he would sleep at all but surprised himself by falling into a long, deep slumber as soon as he lay down.

Waking many hours later, he allowed Tatillion to wash and shave him, and to lay out his clothes. The manservant also insisted that he eat—another luxury de Lacey had not allowed himself since before the holdup. But everything he did, every action he took was quick and curtailed; his only thought was to return to Eugenie's house, to her side, and to see her lovely blue eyes open, and to hear her melodic voice.

On arrival at the house, he was ushered up the stairs by the butler, to a large airy room. The light was low, the curtains being mostly drawn. There was a bustle of movement in the room, as a maid and a footman deposited an occasional table and a tea service in front of Madame Ponnette, who was seated beside the bed.

De Lacey bowed to madame, but he had eyes only for Eugenie. He approached the bed to find her still sleeping, her face pale and pinched, her golden hair spread out on the pillow under her head.

Taking her slim hand, he kissed it, holding it to his lips, hoping his warmth would wake her. Eugenie didn't stir. Distressed, he turned to madame, his voice wavering.

"She wasn't shot, madame, was she? Did I miss it? Is she injured?"

Madame smiled sadly and waved him into a chair. "Eugenie suffered some memory loss from the trauma we suffered in traveling to London," she began. "Tea?"

De Lacey blinked at the turn in conversation and replied by rote, "Certainly, thank you."

As she poured, Madame Ponnette continued. "Have you heard about our flight? Amongst the gossips, I mean?"

He smiled grimly, accepting the cup from her. "Of course. Our tales are of special interest to these English."

"Then you will know that Eugenie's lady's maid was shot protecting her."

One of de Lacey's eyebrows raced up. "I knew a maid was killed. I didn't know it was in the protection of Mademoiselle Ponnette."

"Yes. Lillie pushed Eugenie into a copse but was sadly left in the firing line herself." Madame Ponnette's eyes glistened.

"Does Eugenie blame herself for the death?"

Madame Ponnette frowned. "I don't know. It was quite strange. When we arrived at the boat that was to take us across the channel, Eugenie was laughing and euphoric. It was as if none of the tragedy had occurred, in her own mind Lillie was still alive, as was her dear *papa*." At this, Madame Ponnette drew a kerchief from the side of her chair and held it to her nose, before continuing in a choked voice. "She had gone into the city to visit a friend, and her journey home took her past the Abbaye. She found herself caught up in the middle of them." A waver of hysteria passed through Madame Ponnette's voice, and she gulped.

De Lacey reached out to cover Madame Ponnette's hand with his own, and she smiled through her tears. "Her father was murdered there, at the prison."

A wave of nausea descended on him. He had only heard reports of the massacres, but they had been bloody and graphic. Stories of corpses mutilated, beheaded and mocked, of gross inhumanity. "Did she actually see…?"

"Yes," madame dipped her head, pain etched across her face. "I had gone to find her, and I saw it too. It was horrendous. There was nothing left of poor Maurice when they were done. He was cut to ribbons. Eugenie made the mistake of berating the crowd for their deeds and consigning them to hell. She was pointed out as a traitor to the republic."

De Lacey nodded, his stomach dropping further. He knew the treatment meted out to traitors. Swift, harsh judgment and execution. "So that explains why you were forced to leave."

"Precisely. And while we got away, Eugenie has been left with sizeable gaps in her recall, and nightmares in place of her memories."

De Lacey glanced over at Eugenie's still figure and frowned. "Very well, but that doesn't explain why she is still asleep now."

Eugenie murmured, and they both jumped up, hurrying to her side. However, she was only fretting in her sleep. A slight frown crossed her brow, and de Lacey trailed his hand across it and down her cheek. "Rest now, little one. Don't despair." She seemed to relax, her breathing deeper.

Madame Ponnette gave a gentle, tired smile that reached into her eyes, making them sparkle in the dim light. "She responds to you, vicomte."

"I only wish she would respond more," he replied.

"She will come out of this in her own time," soothed madame, returning to her chair. "The doctors warned me that any excitement could bring the memories flooding back. And when they did, the doctors did not know how her mind might respond. They said she might develop a nervous tic or permanent trembling in her hands. They mentioned that perhaps her body would shut down altogether. When Doctor Moore came yesterday, he said her body was just trying to catch up with her mind, and that when the two were fully acquainted again, she would wake."

De Lacey threw a glance at the widow. "And how long did the good doctor suggest this transformation would take?"

Madame Ponnette shook her head in a tired gesture. "He said there was a possibility she might never wake."

He digested this information in silence. Eugenie might never wake? But she must. His heart would never survive her loss. Unbidden tears came to his eyes, and he leaned over the sleeping Eugenie to keep her mother from seeing them.

"I do think that Eugenie's responding to your touch is a positive sign though." Madame Ponnette's voice carried a ray of hope. "The doctor told us to stay connected to her—to touch her and talk to her. Perhaps in a dark corner of her mind, something one of us says or does will reach her, and she will return to us." Madame's smile slipped, and a paroxysm of grief crossed her brow. After a moment, she took a deep, shuddering breath and said, "It is devastating to see one's own child in such a state and be able to do nothing about it."

De Lacey agreed. The frustration of sitting and watching and waiting was enough to drive anyone to distraction. He knew he could not stay away, yet he wasn't sure of his welcome. Still, he had no choice but to ask. If she didn't allow it, he would wait in the parlor, or out on the street. De Lacey returned to sit down beside Madame Ponnette again and took her hand. "Madame, I know it is a little outside the bounds of propriety, but do you mind if I stay? To watch over Eugenie?"

"Of course not, vicomte. You told me your feelings for my daughter only yesterday."

De Lacey was surprised for a moment. Was it only yesterday he had traveled headlong to her rescue? The days and nights blurred together, but there was one thing he specifically wanted Eugenie's mother to know about her brave daughter.

"Madame, despite my traveling to save her, you should know by the time I found her, she was quite adeptly organizing her own escape. She is a truly remarkable woman."

A smile returned to the widow's face. "Thank you, vicomte."

"Please, call me Jean. Or de Lacey. I do not feel much like a vicomte at the moment."

"Nor do I feel like a baroness. Just a mother, grieving a husband and daughter." She sighed heavily and rose to her feet. De Lacey made to rise as well, but she pushed him back down with a hand on his shoulder. "I've been here for hours, just staring at my beautiful girl's face, waiting for any sign. I feel as if I am going out of my mind. Do you mind sitting with her for a little while? I need to get some rest. Though goodness knows if I will even be able to close my eyes."

"I will watch over her as closely as you yourself would," de Lacey promised, clasping Madame Ponnette's hand in his own. She squeezed and let go, turning to leave the room.

"If you need anything, the butler and maids are taking it in turns to be available at all times. You need only pull the bell."

"Thank you, madame."

"Goodnight Jean. And bless you." She eased the door closed as she left.

De Lacey turned back to the beauty lying in the bed, silent as the grave. The bed clothes and linens were pure white, Eugenie's hair laying as spun gold over them. De Lacey reached to let a skein fall through his fingers, before skimming the back of his hand across her pale cheek and dropping a chaste kiss there.

"Wherever you are, come back to me, *chérie*," he whispered, allowing his tears to fall freely. "I will be waiting right here beside you."

CHAPTER THIRTY-ONE

Eugenie's first waking sensation was the shock of cold. Someone had pressed a goblet to her lips and poured a tiny bit of water into her mouth. She gulped the liquid, the water a blessed coolness against her parched throat.

"More," she croaked.

"Eugenie?" She sensed movement and then her hand was grasped in two large, warm palms. The voice was familiar, but her foggy brain couldn't place it.

"More water."

Another trickle, that she guzzled as though it were the elixir of life. She whimpered, wondering why her limbs were heavy, and her eyes refused to open.

"More."

"I can't give you more, *chérie*. Not until you are sitting up. You'll choke on it otherwise."

She vaguely registered that she was in a warm, comfortable bed and her tired mind was content to dwell in that happy place for a moment before with a start, all her memories returned.

She struggled to sit up but was held back by a pair of gentle but forceful hands.

"Relax *chérie*. You are safe."

She blinked in the half light, and her nursemaid came into focus, standing awkwardly beside her bed.

"De Lacey?" Of all the people she expected to see, he would never have counted amongst them. Why was he here?

"Yes, it's me."

"Where is *maman*?"

"Rachel went to fetch her, the very moment you stirred. She'll be here directly. Now, do you think you can sit up?"

"Of course," Eugenie replied with asperity, only to be frustrated by her own recalcitrant limbs. "Why won't my arms work?"

"You've been asleep for a while, *chérie*." Eugenie's brows twitched at the endearment, but she let it pass. De Lacey leaned over her and Eugenie cringed back, until she realized he was offering his arms to help her to a sitting position.

She blushed. It wasn't every day a young woman had a gentleman in her room, and in such a state. Her silken chemise pulled tight over her chest as she sat up, emphasizing the curve of her breast. Eugenie made sure not to catch his eye and loosened the garment at the first opportunity.

"My baby girl!" The door flung open with a bang, and Madame Ponnette rushed into the room, embracing her daughter. "Oh, *ma bibiche*, we've been so worried! *Dieu merci*, you're awake!"

"What do you mean, *maman*?" Eugenie was confused.

"Why my dear, you've been asleep for almost a week!

"A week?" Once again Eugenie tried to sit upright, but she fell back against the pillows, frustrated and defeated.

"What do you remember, *chérie*?" asked de Lacey gently.

Eugenie closed her eyes as the avalanche of memories crashed into her again. "I remember my father is dead," she said quietly, and her mother gripped her hand. "I know I watched it happen, and I know I am responsible for our misfortunes."

"It is not your fault, *mon cœur*," soothed her mother.

"No, but it is," argued Eugenie. "If I had stayed quiet, none of this would have happened."

"But had you stayed quiet, you would not have been my Eugenie." Her mother's proud, sad smile brought tears to Eugenie's eyes. "You might resemble me a little on the outside, but inside, you are all your father's daughter."

Eugenie felt a twinge of hurt. "*Maman*, why didn't you tell me? Why didn't you remind me?"

Eugenie's mother spread her hands wide at her daughter's reproach.

"The doctors, they told us not to, that the shock might be too much for you. They assured us that you should regain your memories in time. And if you didn't, they said the memories were too traumatic for you to remember, and that you would be better not to recall them." Her mother's lip trembled, and she clasped both of Eugenie's hands in hers. "I ached to tell you, *chérie*. Especially when you woke from a nightmare calling for your *papa*. When you insisted he was still alive and that we weren't doing enough to save him."

Tears welled in Eugenie's eyes. "Oh, *maman*. To think of the sadness and grief you've had to endure alone."

"I've survived. We Ponnettes are survivors." She said it with sad, lonely pride, and Eugenie's heart swelled.

"Now," her mother said, slapping her hands down on her lap and standing up. "Jean has been here beside you the whole time, *mon cœur*, except for those moments when I sent him home to sleep and bathe. I do believe he has something to ask you." She stood up from the bed, smiling down at her daughter. "I can't tell you how pleased I am, *chérie*." She kissed her fingers and pressed them to Eugenie's forehead, before exiting the room.

De Lacey claimed her place on the bed, taking Eugenie's hand, and she frowned.

"What actually happened, Jean?"

"What do you remember, ma *chérie*?"

She shook her head, perplexed. "I recall walking in the park with Rachel and then a woman blindfolding and gagging me. We drove for hours and hours." Eugenie's eyes widened as she recalled another detail. "Oh, there was another captive in the coach, only I think they disposed of him a short way out of London. Did you find him? Is he dead?"

De Lacey patted her hand in comfort. "That was Jack, Maggie's brother. He's safe."

"Maggie, that was her name." Eugenie nodded. "We arrived at a barn in the early morning, and she left me there. I remember being dreadfully thirsty and feeling as if I was the only person in the world." Her brow furrowed. "After that, I don't remember very much at all, until waking here."

"Do you want to know?"

Eugenie thought for a moment then nodded, her brows still drawn, but a look of resigned apprehension on her fine features. "Yes. I believe I do."

So, de Lacey told her of his flight from London, of finding Maggie and then Eugenie herself, and of Ben's untimely death, along with the gunshot that triggered Eugenie's coma.

"I thought for a moment you had been shot, *ma chérie*. You were so pale and still. But we found no wound on you. It wasn't until we arrived back in London that your *maman* told me about your condition. Those hours on the road from the inn to London were torturous—not knowing what was wrong with you, and having no power to help." He drew a long, shaky breath and his fingers tightened around Eugenie's. "I wanted to tell you something. Something I should have told you long ago. I didn't believe someone like me, someone so jaded and brittle, could feel what I was feeling. But these past few days, I never thought I'd smile again until you were safe and well." He smiled, a tremulous, unsure smile and Eugenie could only smile back, raising one eyebrow.

"A grand passion, monsieur? Is that what you feel?"

"More," he said confidently, taking both of her hands and kissing them fervently. "I love you with every part of me. I love all that I've seen of you—your wit and your dignity and your strength. I want to know the rest of you, Eugenie, and I want to take the rest of my life to do so. *Ma chérie*, will you make me the happiest man on earth and marry me?"

Eugenie's heart did a quick flip. Then her shoulders slumped.

"No, monsieur. I cannot."

CHAPTER THIRTY-TWO

It mattered not how much he pleaded his undying affection, Eugenie was resolute.

"You would not be good for me, monsieur. You say you love me, but I cannot believe it. And I've told you before; I will have nothing but a love match."

"But this is a love match," insisted de Lacey. "I love you. And you love me."

"And how many others do you love, monsieur?" Eugenie's eyes flashed fire, even though her voice was cold. "Your tavern whore in Kent? Your lover in Southwall Street? And me as well? Oh, no, monsieur, I will not be treated thus." Eugenie fell back against the pillows, all her energy spent in the tirade.

De Lacey didn't know how to answer. How had Eugenie found out about his lover? And exactly how was he to explain that he had left them both behind?

"They are in the past, *ma chérie*," he said soothingly. "You are my only love for the future."

Weakly, Eugenie continued as if she hadn't heard him. "And what about your other activities, *hein?* Smuggling? A couple of bottles of brandy is one thing, monsieur. But when you are part of the gang, running with low men and criminals..."

"I've given that away, Eugenie. You must believe me."

But she wouldn't listen, turning her head away, no matter how many protestations he made, or kisses he placed on her.

She raised her voice, just a little. "Go away, Jean. I have a headache."

Eugenie's maid, Rachel, barreled into the room, carrying a pitcher of water, and scowling at de Lacey, followed by Isabeau who jumped on Eugenie's bed and regarded de Lacey out of belligerent, yellow cat's eyes. Directly behind the cat, Lord Underwood also strolled in, looking supremely uncomfortable.

"I do think it would be better if you were to leave Eugenie to rest now, monsieur," said the older man, taking de Lacey's arm and pulling him out of the room. De Lacey could see the sympathy in the other man's eyes, as he shut the door behind him.

"You've set yourself quite a task there, monsieur," Lord Underwood chuckled. "Once their mind is set, it's not easy to change it. The flaw runs through all the females in her family."

"What's to be done?" said de Lacey, his hands threading through his hair. He raised his desperate glance to Lord Underwood.

"Give her time," the older man urged, gently leading him down the stairs. "Maybe when she's recovered she might see things in a different light."

De Lacey heaved a heavy sigh and smiled his thanks at the other man as he was gently but firmly shown the door.

CHAPTER THIRTY-THREE

Eugenie couldn't stop her tears from falling. He was gone.

Her mother bustled back into the room, a look of deep concern on her face. "*Chérie!* You refused him?"

"I did, *maman.*"

"But why?" Her mother's voice squeaked and her hands, never still, opened wide. "He loves you; he was here for you the whole time…"

"Because he is a smuggler."

Her mother raised one eyebrow.

"And because he doesn't only love me, *maman.* And I can't bear to share him."

Madame Ponnette frowned. "He is pursuing another?"

"He has a lover."

Understanding flashed across her mother's face. After a moment, she replied quietly, "It is accepted that a man will have a lover, *chérie.*"

"I cannot accept it." Eugenie's tear-stained expression was steadfast, although her lip was quivering. "It would only bring heartache to start down such a road."

There was a long silence. Eugenie's mother toyed with the tassels on her shawl, her face shadowed.

"Do you love him?" Her mother sat on Eugenie's bed, and turned her blue-green eyes on her, studying her daughter's face.

"More than anything." Eugenie buried her face in her hands.

"Oh, *mon cœur.*" The widow drew herself up to take her

daughter in her arms, but after a moment, Eugenie shook her off with a scowl.

"No! I will not be pitied. I'm—how do they say here?—sticking to my guns on this one." She nodded fiercely.

A frown crossed her mother's brow. "Is there nothing that would change your mind?"

Eugenie shrugged. "Maybe if he were to change his character?" She half-smiled at her mother. "But we all know that is not possible."

Madame Ponnette looked down at her hands for a long moment before asking meekly, "Could you not overlook his impulses, *chérie*? After all, he is only a man."

"*Non, maman*, I must be firm. I do not wish to be merely a pretty ornament for de Lacey to carry around to be appreciated when he chooses. We have already discussed this."

"*Vraiment?*" Her mother was surprised and suddenly deeply interested. "And when did this discussion take place?"

Eugenie blushed. "It is of no consequence, *maman*. I have made my position clear to de Lacey. He knows I will not accept his offer unless he is prepared to take me and only me. And until he can prove his devotion as well as his love, I can not accept his offer."

Her mother sighed and glanced sideways at her. "I shall continue to pray for your happiness, *mon cœur*. However, I must say, in my estimation, you will not do better than Vicomte Landreville."

"Then pray for his complete change in character, *maman*, for that is the only way we shall ever be together."

CHAPTER THIRTY-FOUR

"I do not know how a man can go from the heights of elation to the depths of despair in such a short amount of time," sighed de Lacey from his comfortable chair at Brooks's, staring into his fifth brandy. "It was as if she was delivered up into my arms, then taken from me, all in one short hour." He brought his fingertips to his lips and kissed them, then gestured off into the air.

While de Lacey was grateful for the sympathy apparent in Lord Edenburgh's face, he knew his friend was close to reaching the end of his patience. After all, de Lacey had done nothing but talk about Eugenie for the past several days. He gave a weak chuckle.

"*Mon ami*, I am pathetic, no? Who would have ever thought that I, Jean de Lacey, lover extraordinaire, would be brought low by a chit of a woman who knows not what is good for her?"

His friend sighed and drew his pipe from his inner pocket, stuffing it with tobacco and tamping it down. Placing the stem between his teeth, he lit a match before responding to de Lacey's words.

"I've known you for many years, my friend, and I say this with the greatest of affection. Yes. You are pathetic."

De Lacey chose not to hear him. "She wouldn't have me because I was a criminal. A criminal, Quincey. Me! In Paris, I was a celebrated lawyer."

Lord Edenburgh chuckled, sending little puffs of smoke from his mouth. "In some circles, they are considered one and the same," he replied with a wink.

De Lacey replied irritably, "Quincey, please."

His friend was immediately chastised. "Apologies my friend. You were saying?"

De Lacey was suspicious of the twinkle in the earl's eyes, but he continued, "Yes—and even when I explained, she still wouldn't listen."

"Yes. You've already told me. Several times over."

"Why won't she believe me?"

"Probably because you've spent the past few months studiously lying to her."

Again, de Lacey chose to ignore his friend's words. "And then there's the matter of my lover."

"Ah, yes, your lover." Lord Edenburgh settled back into his winged chair, a visage of patient resignation noticeable through the cigar smoke.

"It is not a crime to have a paramour! But Eugenie, she insists she will be my only love or not at all. She drives me to insanity." De Lacey downed the rest of his brandy in one gulp. "Does she not realize I have no desire for another woman? That I haven't seen Juliet in weeks?"

Lord Edenburgh's eyebrow twitched up. "Apparently not."

"What can I do to convince her?"

De Lacey had asked the question rhetorically; however, Lord Edenburgh spoke up, as an idea occurred to him.

"Sometimes the ladies get it into their heads that it is shameful as a wife to have a husband with a mistress. Perhaps she wants to enter marriage with a clean slate."

De Lacey threw his friend a questioning glance. "I do not understand this saying—a clean slate. What does that mean, *mon ami*?"

Lord Edenburgh seemed to warm to his topic, leaning forward eagerly. "Yes, she does not wish her marriage bed to be shared with another. Figuratively, of course."

"But neither do I wish it, Quincey."

The earl went on expounding, "So, you could tell her that you have given up dalliances, but only do so until the fancy strikes you again."

De Lacey shook his head. "I could never do that."

Lord Edenburgh looked skyward as if asking heaven for assistance. "Why the devil not?"

"I could never tell her such a falsehood." And that was one of the problems. How much easier it all would be if he could lie to her!

"Then from where I am sitting, you have two choices. Either agree to her terms and never sleep with another woman ever again or don't agree to her terms and give her up." Lord Edenburgh slumped back in his chair and took a great puff on his pipe as if he was exhausted.

"Well, that's simple. I shall give up other women."

"You?"

"Of course." De Lacey was mildly outraged. "I can control my desires as well as the next gentleman. Just because I have chosen not to in the past..." He left the statement hanging.

"So, have you told her you are planning undying devotion to her?"

De Lacey deflated a little. "No, I suppose I have not. Not in as many words, anyway." He dwelled on the thought for a moment, before his indignation swelled anew. "But the smuggling! I have told her I am no longer a part of it. She refuses to believe me."

"Why do you think she would do that?"

De Lacey's shoulders fell. "I suppose I have given her no reason to trust me." He dropped his head into his hands. "I wish I had never met those men," he groaned.

His friend regarded him shrewdly for a long moment. "You know all you needed to do was to refuse to be involved with the smugglers following your escape to England?"

"I know."

"And swallowed your stupid French pride and asked for help?"

"I know."

"And you know she had every right to refuse you when it was your friends who abducted her."

"*Mon dieu*, Quincey, I know," De Lacey snapped, then buried

187

his face in his hands. The brandy glass swayed in his lax fingers, and Lord Edenburgh leaned over and relieved him of it, returning it to the table.

"How can I make her believe me?" He glanced up through his fingers to catch a calculating expression on his friend's face. "What are you thinking?"

The earl's features returned to their normal, good-natured expression. "I have no idea what you mean, my friend."

"That face." De Lacey pointed unsteadily at him, his eyes narrowing in suspicion. "I've seen that face before. You are up to something."

Lord Edenburgh's expression changed again, to one of cherubic innocence. "I am up to no such thing."

De Lacey continued to point at him until his finger began to waver, and he dropped his hand into his lap. "It's no use," he sighed. "I don't know how else to woo her."

"My friend, tell me in all honesty. Is this a passing phase? Or do you truly want to spend the rest of your life tied to this one woman?"

De Lacey scowled. "You ask such a question when you see me in such straits as these?" He swept his hand down the side of his body. "Drunk, disheveled, and desperate?"

"My dear, I've seen you in such straits before," chuckled Quincey. "Remember Brussels?"

"I'm serious, Quincey. I love this woman. More than any woman I've ever known before. And if I can't win her, I don't know what I will do." With these dramatic words, de Lacey threw an arm in the air. The gesture was quickly followed by the arrival of the butler, Markham.

"Markham, bring me more brandy."

"Yes, monsieur," replied the butler smoothly, nodding very slightly at Quincey's shake of his head. He walked away.

"Don't you think you've had enough?" asked the earl.

"What else is there to do when my love lies not two miles away, yet I can't even see her?" His friend sighed.

"I can't believe I am telling you this, de Lacey, but you might be well served to cut all ties with your lover publicly."

"To what end?"

"So word gets around, de Lacey. So your Mademoiselle Ponnette hears that you have turned over a new leaf." He spoke slowly and deliberately as if he thought de Lacey was a simpleton.

"And I have, *mon ami*," cried de Lacey, grasping his friend's hand. "That is what I have done. Turned over a new leaf."

"Good for you," replied the earl sourly, releasing his hand from de Lacey's grip.

De Lacey didn't hear him. "And so Eugenie will know that I will be faithful only to her?"

"Now, now, dear fellow, let's not make any promises we can't keep. Let's just say that she will know you are serious about matrimony." He almost shuddered with the word.

De Lacey smiled with pity at his friend. "I am serious about matrimony, *mon ami*. You do not know what it is to be in love. It is the greatest emotion ever. And the worst. But mostly the greatest." His friend raised one disbelieving eyebrow at him, and de Lacey laughed. "You'll see. One day, love will come to you, when you least expect it."

"I sincerely doubt it."

De Lacey's equanimity lasted for only a moment, as his thoughts returned to his own situation. "But she still believes me to be a criminal," he said.

The crafty look returned to the earl's face. "One step at a time, old fellow."

Confused by the look, de Lacey chose to ignore, once again. "Do you really think Eugenie would hear the gossip? That she would hear I was free?"

"Of course," the earl replied confidently. "All women gossip. It's built into their natures. Mademoiselle Ponnette could not help but hear."

De Lacey jumped up out of his chair. "In that case, I shall repair to her house immediately. She will know how to put the word around." He grabbed the earl's hand, pumping it enthusiastically. *"Mon ami*, I can't thank you enough."

"Oh, I think you can, my friend. I think you can."

De Lacey stared at him for a moment, the meaning of his cryptic utterance lost on him. Then, a fog of brandy and good intentions descended again, and he almost flew out of the room, intent on his new crusade.

CHAPTER THIRTY-FIVE

Seated in the morning room, Eugenie offered up a huge sigh. Despite the bright early afternoon sunshine spilling into the room, she was not able to find any enjoyment in the usual pastime of receiving guests. Still, she smiled on the few guests who found their way to Lady Underwood's home, making them welcome, and keeping herself busy with pouring the tea. She had been glad to see Felicity today. Felicity was, of course, privy to all her secrets, and she felt as if she needed a quiet conversation to get all the silly thoughts of Vicomte Landreville out of her head. Felicity had frankly told her she was mad to have refused the vicomte, but Eugenie was still sticking to her guns.

"The Earl of Edenburgh."

She shared a startled glance with her mother. What on earth was the Earl of Edenburgh doing visiting here? Then she looked to Felicity, whose face had turned rosy at the mention of him.

The gentleman was ushered into the room, and Lady Underwood stood and smiled. "My lord, welcome. Please, take a seat." But despite her gracious tone of voice, Eugenie could see she was aching with curiosity as to why the earl might be at her home.

He sat, then looked around at who was in the room. Eugenie noticed he started a little at seeing Felicity, before nodding at her. She nodded in return. It was odd. They were childhood friends. Eugenie hoped there was no falling out between them. They had seemed so cozy at the ball.

"Can Eugenie pour you some tea, my lord?" Lady Underwood played the hostess to perfection.

"My thanks, Lady Underwood; however, I was hoping for a private word with Mademoiselle Ponnette."

"A private word?" Eugenie's mother broke in, and Eugenie hid a smile as the earl blushed beet red, as did Felicity.

"Not like that. I mean, lovely girl and all that, ma'am, all credit to you, but I'm not in the marrying line."

"Oh? Then you won't mind if I were to accompany my daughter while you hold this private word with her?" Madame Ponnette's tone brooked little opposition.

"Of course. Only, it's a matter of some delicacy." The earl produced a handkerchief from about his person and mopped his brow. His color hadn't receded, and Eugenie thought he couldn't have been more uncomfortable if he'd tried.

"Indeed? Should I be concerned?"

"No, madame, not at all."

"Hmm." Madame Ponnette made a show of deciding whether she would permit a *tête-à-tête* with Eugenie. Eugenie eyed her mother askance and turned to the earl.

"I should be happy to speak with you, my lord. Shall we repair to the parlor?" She stood and gracefully made her way past the earl, scowling at her mother who smiled innocently and walked across the hallway. The earl hesitated for a moment, looking between the two Ponnette ladies before he hurriedly bowed and rushed after Eugenie.

"I do apologize for my mother, my lord," she said, hearing muffled laughter from the morning room. "She is sometimes a little too protective of my virtue."

"Understandably so," replied the earl, looking her over with the expression of a connoisseur. Eugenie waited until his eyes returned to her face, then gave him an unimpressed look. He colored again. "Do excuse me. Force of habit."

"Won't you sit down?"

Lord Edenburgh sat in the nearest chair, and Eugenie took another close by. "Now, what was it you wished to speak to me about?"

The earl scratched behind his ear, looked longingly out of the parlor window, and fidgeted with his cravat pin and his cuffs before he stammered, "I need to talk to you about de Lacey."

"De Lacey?"

"Yes."

Eugenie waited for him to say more, but in the silence that followed his words, she said, "Well, what about him?"

"He's pining over you, and I want to put an end to it."

She found herself unaccountably pleased by the earl's words. De Lacey was pining over her. That could only be a good sign.

"How do you expect to do that, my lord?"

"I was hoping you would do it." The earl leaned forward in his chair, his expression earnest. "You love him, don't you? Because he loves you to distraction. It's nauseating, actually."

Eugenie frowned. "Whether I love him or not is entirely my business, my lord, and not yours."

"I'm quite aware. And de Lacey's feelings for you should be between he and you. I don't want to be involved." The earl shuddered. "Dashed ugly business, marriage. Only every time I see him he's waxing lyrical about you and how wonderful you are and how heartless. Had he gotten over it, I should certainly not have bothered you. I have nursed several of my friends through broken hearts, and I thought I would be doing the same for poor de Lacey. But his heart will not be unbroken, mademoiselle."

Eugenie smiled sadly. "Unfortunately, the question is not whether he loves me or not. I have no doubt that he does."

"Then why do you refuse him?"

"There are two reasons..."

The earl snapped his fingers, and Eugenie stopped, startled.

"It's the smuggling, is it not? Well, I can tell you without any doubt that he has left that life behind."

"I find that very hard to believe, my lord."

"Whether you do or don't, it is true. They nearly killed him for it."

Eugenie thought back to the day when de Lacey appeared at the ball only to almost topple over in a faint. "Did they hurt him?" she asked in dawning horror.

"Oh yes. They beat him up, and they were going to shoot him."

Eugenie's eyes were wide. "What happened?"

Lord Edenburgh produced a little smile at his secret. "Let's just say the magistrate of the area is a particular friend of de Lacey's. He bargained for de Lacey's life. Successfully it seems."

"Oh, *merci*." Eugenie was up out of her chair and had her arms thrown around the earl before he could move. This was the kind of proof she was seeking. Her heart lightened as one of her concerns was nullified.

"I didn't say the magistrate was me."

"Oh." Eugenie stood back, her face flaming.

"But it was." He grinned at her. "So, you may continue to embrace me."

Eugenie had to laugh. The earl was incorrigible. "Maybe some other time, my lord," she replied, hastening to return to her seat. "But why did he not tell me?"

The earl shrugged. "Maybe because the story doesn't place him in a particularly good light?"

"That doesn't matter to me."

"It matters to him."

Eugenie's mother came into the room, evidently thinking that the meeting between Eugenie and the earl had gone on long enough. The earl immediately sat upright in his chair, like a schoolboy facing a fearsome schoolmarm.

"I trust your business with my daughter has concluded successfully, my lord?" she asked sweetly.

The earl recognized he was being asked to leave. He might be a powerful man in London, but against the ferocity of a mother, he was no match. "Certainly, madame. Well, concluded for the present, anyway." He looked at Eugenie. "You will give the matter more thought, will you not, mademoiselle?"

"I certainly shall, my lord."

He seemed satisfied with this answer, nodding and saying, "In that case, I wish you both good day." He walked out of the room, whistling as he picked up his hat and coat and was shown out of the house.

Eugenie and her mother looked into each others' eyes and burst into laughter.

"He is certainly a character," said Eugenie.

"What did he want?" Her mother took a chair and urged Eugenie into another.

"He wanted to prove to me that de Lacey wasn't smuggling anymore." Eugenie looked out of the window, deep in thought.

"And was he able to prove it to you?"

Her eyes returned to her mother. "Oh yes. Only..."

"Only..."

Eugenie gave a dissatisfied shrug, her brows drawing together. "He still has a lover."

Her mother took her hand. "You must do what is right for you, *ma chérie*."

After a moment's hesitation, she nodded, although her words were tinged with sadness. "In that case, I still cannot marry him."

CHAPTER THIRTY-SIX

The following morning at breakfast, Eugenie was surprised when a footman came to stand beside her, holding a note on a silver tray. A greater surprise was that it was from Lady Juliet Hampshire, asking her to take a turn around the park later that morning.

Eugenie certainly didn't consider Lady Hampshire a good friend—more of an acquaintance. Curious as to why the lady would request such a thing, Eugenie dashed off her own reply to say she would meet her at the entrance to the park in an hour's time.

Hyde Park was the meeting place for all of upper society. Some chose to ride in curricles and open vehicles so they could acknowledge their acquaintances without feeling the need to stop. Others walked or even rode.

Eugenie, with an attentive Rachel by her side, watched as Lady Hampshire stepped down from a coach and gave instructions to her coachman. She wore a lovely blue velvet coat trimmed with what Eugenie supposed was ermine and carried an ermine muff. A long white feather swayed above her dark blue turban, which set off her auburn curls delightfully.

"My dear Mademoiselle Ponnette, I am so pleased you could make the time for me," she said as she approached.

"I must say, your note left me curious," replied Eugenie with a smile "I felt I had no choice but to assuage my curiosity."

Lady Hampshire's tinkling laugh filled the air. "Wonderful. Let us wander the trails then, shall we?"

They moved forward, Rachel and a man who must have been Lady Hampshire's footman following at a distance that allowed private conversation.

To begin with, Lady Hampshire seemed to want to discuss the beauty of the day, the various flowers and plants they passed as they walked, and the grist that made up the gossip mill. But at length, she silenced, and Eugenie knew she had come to whatever it was she had been planning to say from the beginning.

"This is a little difficult for me," Lady Hampshire confessed with a short laugh. "I do not wish to damage myself in your estimation, and yet what I have to tell you can only accomplish just that."

Eugenie replied in surprise, "I don't understand. Damage you in my estimation? How on earth could you accomplish such a thing? We are barely even acquainted."

"And yet, I feel as if I know you very well indeed," murmured Lady Hampshire. She reached into her muff and withdrew a folded letter. Eugenie noticed that her hands shook as she gave it to her.

"It's only a short missive," she said, "Would you read it as we walk along?"

Intrigued, Eugenie opened the letter.

My dear Mademoiselle Ponnette,

So, it is time to reveal my secret. Jean de Lacey used to be my lover. You will note, I say used to be. He is no longer mine.

He has never really loved me, mademoiselle. I reminded him of someone else he lost, that is all. You, on the other hand, have captured his heart and soul, made him forget this phantom he was holding on to, and I couldn't be more pleased for both of you.

Treat him gently, mademoiselle. He is but a man and those of us with experience know that sometimes, they can be as stupid as sheep. However, they are very rarely unkind on purpose, and in this case, when Jean loves you so dearly, I do believe he will try everything to secure your happiness.

Juliet, Lady Hampshire.

Her thoughts in a whirl, Eugenie folded the letter.

"You need not speak further to me if that is your preference," started Lady Hampshire, but Eugenie shook her head.

"No, on the contrary, I am pleased with your confidence." A smile crossed her face. "Very pleased indeed."

Lady Hampshire seemed confused. "You do not hate me? Or think I am wanton?"

Eugenie frowned. "No indeed. As a widow, you are permitted discreet affairs. And since I had never heard your name linked with de Lacey, I can only believe it was discreet." She laughed. "Of course, I am hideously jealous of you, and will be doing my utmost to remove from my mind any thought of the two of you together."

"That is understood," replied Lady Hampshire with a small smile.

Eugenie licked her lips in nervous gesture. "I have only one question, my Lady, which I pray you will answer honestly and openly."

"Certainly, if it is within my power."

Eugenie drew in a deep breath. "Do you believe he will be faithful to me?"

Lady Hampshire considered for a moment before answering. "I do believe it," she said slowly. "I think, despite the stories bandied about, that when de Lacey settles his heart on someone, he is a one-woman man."

Eugenie smiled broadly and gave the startled lady a quick embrace. "Thank you. That is all that concerned me."

Eugenie sighed as de Lacey entered her aunt's morning room, allowing herself a moment to be enraptured by him. So handsome, polished, and stylish, but just a tiny bit frayed. Both physically and emotionally. The instant he crossed the threshold, he sought out her eyes, a hopeful, pleading expression in his own. She looked back at him steadily.

Isabeau appeared out of nowhere, offering de Lacey a vocal welcome. It seemed the black and white cat recognized the sound of de Lacey's footsteps, and she was insistent in getting her share of his attention, winding herself around his legs and mewing pitifully until he leaned down to stroke her silky fur. She escorted him further into the morning room; her tail held high. Eugenie had to smile at her pet. It seemed that Isabeau indeed had good taste in men.

"Eugenie, why don't you show the vicomte to the parlor?" Her mother was smiling broadly, and Eugenie flushed.

On reaching the room, de Lacey turned and, as Isabeau skittered in, closed the door behind her. Then he lunged toward Eugenie, capturing her in his arms, and dropping his lips on to hers.

For a moment, her thoughts were muddled by the taste and smell of de Lacey. She allowed him to ravish her mouth, unsure that she could ever stop, reveling in the delicious sensations he was causing in her body. His hands wandered the curve of her spine, then up her arms to her shoulders, to cup her face. He only broke the kiss long enough to breathe, "Eugenie," before his lips captured hers again.

However, that one word was enough to bring Eugenie back to the present. She disengaged herself from his grasp, striding away and standing behind a chair as if it would offer her protection.

"Just before we do this, I have one question."

"Only one?" His green eyes sparkled, and she tried to be severe with him.

"Did you ask Lady Hampshire to write that letter?"

"What letter?"

"She wrote me a letter."

"Did she now? Interesting." Eugenie could see de Lacey's discomfort as he wondered exactly what Lady Hampshire had said. She let him suffer for a few moments, before putting him out of his misery.

"It was a good letter."

She moved toward him, and he seemed to realize the same pull as she. In the center of the room, they came to stand, face to face, their bodies so close, not daring to touch. She licked her lips. His gaze sharpened on them, and Eugenie noted with satisfaction the harsh breath he took in.

"Kiss me."

He reached for her, and his lips came down to meet hers. Around the couple, the light softened, and the furniture took on soft lines as if it were fading away. Only they existed in the entire world, only his eyes fixed firmly on her lips, this moment...

Then they were yanked back to reality by an unruly yowl and hiss from the window as Isabeau took offense at a dog trawling the street outside and threw herself at the window, intent on teaching the dog some manners. Her tail expanded to twice its size. She scrabbled off the chaise in the window and went to hide in the heavy drapes. Eugenie and de Lacey could hear her quietly grumbling to herself as she settled in her hideaway.

The two of them looked at each other and burst into laughter before Eugenie stood on tiptoes and placed a kiss on her love's lips. Surprised, he jerked back a little, before pulling Eugenie close and deepening the intimate connection.

The kiss was delicious. Eugenie felt lightheaded as de Lacey pressed his tongue against her lips, and she opened, to have him invade her mouth. She tried to copy his movements, their tongues waging a war that no one would win, and that no one wanted to win. The warfare was hot and wet, and Eugenie couldn't help but moan into de Lacey's mouth, which only served to inspire him to drag her even closer, to kiss her even deeper.

Breathless, they pulled back for a moment. "Eugenie," breathed de Lacey. "You must know now that I love you, and only you."

"I know," she replied, hiding her face in the lapels of his coat. "I am sorry I ever doubted you."

"*Ma chérie*, say you will marry me. My heart has been aching to hear you say it."

"Of course I will, Jean. I love you." And their union was sealed with another of the scandalous kisses that made Eugenie's body blush from tip to toe.

CHAPTER THIRTY-SEVEN

The wedding was held a little more than three weeks later, the banns having been read in church each week for three weeks as was proper. De Lacey had wickedly suggested that since they were engaged, they were practically married anyway, so it wasn't really wrong to pre-empt the marriage vows, but Eugenie had been resolute. It had been difficult, the closer and closer her wedding got. Especially when de Lacey pulled her into empty rooms and secluded garden alcoves and kissed her senseless every opportunity he got.

She adored the gown of pale green lawn she and her mother had chosen, cross threaded in gold, and with an open overlay of white silk, also shot through with gold threads and embroidered around the hem in tiny bunches of gold flowers. But she adored her handsome husband much, much more, and seeing the dress crumple into a pile on the floor as de Lacey slowly divested her of it didn't bother her one bit. In fact, she hardly noticed at all.

What she did notice was how deliciously decadent it felt to have de Lacey's hands roaming her body freely, running down her back and then up under her chemise, where he kneaded her buttocks and pulled her close to him. The feel of his manhood against her was intoxicating and unnerving at the same time. He had taken off his coat and waistcoat and his boots and stockings and stood before her in only his shirt and breeches.

His kisses fell against her neck, and she unconsciously tipped her head to the side, her eyelids fluttering closed. The kisses started off as little butterfly kisses, but with each one, his lips met her neck more urgently and became more of a suckle than a kiss until Eugenie yelped.

De Lacey stopped for a moment and regarded her ruefully. "I do apologize, *ma chérie*. I suspect that will leave a mark."

She giggled. "I shall need to wear very high starched collars to ensure nobody notices. But it shall be worth it."

He growled, his eyes dark with passion. "Come here, my wife." He pulled her close again, their lips meeting in a bruising, lustful joust that left Eugenie breathless. De Lacey, without losing eye contact, lifted her off her feet and whirled her around, walking forward until the back of her legs brushed the side of the bed.

Her breath hitched and even as her lower extremities turned molten, a tiny jolt of fear spasmed through her.

De Lacey noticed. "Are you afraid *chérie*?" His voice was gentle and kind, and Eugenie found her eyes filling with tears.

"Of you? Never," she said. De Lacey guided her back on the bed, and she lay, her vision of him becoming wavy through her tears. "Of this? Just a tiny bit, I suppose." She smiled to cover her timidity.

De Lacey sat beside her on the bed, and Eugenie struggled to move to a sitting position. When she had, he took her hand.

"Eugenie, I can't promise it won't hurt. But I can promise I will be as gentle as possible, and I'll do everything I can to make it as painless as I can."

Her smile wavered. "I know," she replied. "Which is why I didn't want to say anything."

"*Chérie*, you must always talk to me," he said, tightening his grip on her hand. "There are no secrets between man and wife. If you are bothered by something, or I do something foolish, you must tell me."

Eugenie's sense of humor resurfaced. "In that case, I'll be telling you often, for you can be very foolish sometimes," she said demurely, a wicked glint in her eye.

De Lacey laughed and pulled her against him, both of them falling back on the bed.

"Oh, ma *chérie*, life will never be dull with you, will it?" He held her circled in his arms and kissed her again, this time slowly, his insistent tongue parting her lips and exploring the inside of her mouth. She had learned the erotic power her tongue held over him during the past three weeks, and she thrust and parried with her own, savoring de Lacey's flavor.

She pushed his shoulder back and straddled him, continuing to kiss him. Their breathing grew ragged together, and Eugenie moaned to feel tiny darts of pleasure zip through her as she rocked her core against de Lacey.

With a sudden movement, he flipped the pair of them over and loomed over her. Eugenie swallowed hard. There was something primal and fierce in his gaze that set her heart thudding in her chest. She knew he was in charge now, that he would take his fill, take her maidenhood. And while the thought still frightened her a little, the sensations she had felt just moments ago awoke a different emotion in her—a need to know how it felt to be filled by a man, to take him inside her, to feel him move. Thinking about it, she felt the moisture start to warm between her legs again.

De Lacey kneeled back and sat Eugenie up a little to remove her chemise, and undid the tie at the waist of her drawers. She lifted her hips a little so he could ease them down. He didn't speak, the only sound, his harsh breathing. She watched him lick his lips as he reached out to caress one of her breasts. The taut nipple tingled at his touch, and Eugenie took a sharp, surprised breath in. He smiled, easing himself back off her legs so he could remove the last of his clothes.

She swallowed when he pulled his shirt off over his head. Long and lean, his muscles were chiseled and strong, his skin bronze in the firelight. Eugenie's eyes strayed to where the v-shaped muscles of his torso disappeared into his breeches. He smiled, noticing where her gaze had drifted.

"Why don't you take these off?" he suggested, a lazy, teasing note in his voice. Eugenie hurried to oblige, eager to see what lay beneath the buff fabric.

She unbuttoned the fall and peeled the breeches down his legs.

Her breath hitched. Right there, just below eye level, his manhood had sprung, sticking out from his body like the thick branch of a magnificent oak. She reached out a hesitant hand, then stopped, looking up into de Lacey's heavy-lidded eyes. With a small nod, he gave her permission to touch.

She ran one finger along the broad shaft, from the glistening tip down to the dark curls between his legs, and back again, fascinated by the tremors she could feel under the silky skin and the gentle pulses she could see. Gathering her courage, she took it in a loosely clasped hand, and again, ran her hand down and back up. She looked up into de Lacey's face. His eyes were closed, but his expression was one of exquisite torture. Eugenie smiled, an odd feeling of power coming over her. Her husband seemed to be enjoying her exploration.

She noticed a bead of moisture collecting at the tip and ran her thumb over it. De Lacey shivered. "Chérie, you have no idea what you do to me," he murmured. "One day, I'm going to show you how to take a man's shaft in your mouth, but right now, all I want to do is bury myself deep in you."

He indicated she should lie on the bed, and she did, watching de Lacey's every action. Like a sinuous tiger, he moved his body over hers, brushing against her and setting every nerve on fire. He straddled her hips, his manhood jutting from him, and he murmured, "Open your legs for me, chérie."

She breathed out and licked her lips, then opened her eyes and looked directly into de Lacey's green ones as she parted her legs. She felt the cool of the room against her hot, wet core. Then, she felt even more.

De Lacey held her womanhood apart with two gentle fingers and pushed the tip of his shaft against her opening, saying as he did, "You are so wonderfully wet, chérie. And so hot." With his thumb, he circled the place she had discovered earlier that sent jabs of exquisite pleasure through her. She started to squirm, feeling his prick at her entrance, feeling urges she had never experienced before, and desperate for de Lacey to meet and fill those urges.

"Jean, I need... I need," she moaned under her breath, and he hushed her.

"I know what you need, *chérie*. Let me give it to you."

With a quick movement he was inside her, and Eugenie cried out loud at the sudden stinging pain in her nether regions.

"Shh," said de Lacey gently. "A moment, *mon amour*. Give it just a moment."

Eugenie breathed quickly, the pain almost too much to bear, but just as de Lacey said, after a moment, it reduced. De Lacey moved inside her, pushing a little further forward and she tensed, but the pain had passed as quickly as it had come.

"I'm alright," she said. "Keep going."

He eased forward until his entire shaft was inside her, then drew back. Eugenie gasped at the feelings coming from her quim. She felt every movement of de Lacey's, all the way through her, and against her body as he pushed completely into her again, this time with a little more force, bumping against her and forcing the breath from her body.

"It is too much, *mon amour*?"

"No, it's not enough," she whispered. De Lacey grinned and sped up his thrusts. Eugenie, realizing de Lacey's ministrations were creating the same sensations that had affected her body before, eagerly joined him, pushing her pelvis up to meet his with each thrust.

She shrieked with the effort of each thrust, her body crying out for release with each smack of de Lacey's skin against hers. The point of her pleasure felt swollen and wet, and she could feel the perspiration between them trickling down her side.

De Lacey roared, throwing his head back and pushing hard into her. With this last thrust against her, she too exploded again, adding her shriek of ecstasy to de Lacey's release.

They lay, spent and breathless, in each other's arms until de Lacey had recovered enough to prop himself up on one elbow to gaze at Eugenie. She lay, sprawled on the bed, shameless under his gaze.

"My beautiful wife, you've made me the happiest of men," he

said, his eyes traveling over her body. "I simply cannot imagine wanting anyone more than I want you."

"You still want me?" she asked. "Even after you've had your fill?"

He growled, laying himself over her again. "I haven't had my fill yet, *ma chérie*. Not even close."

And Eugenie gave a little laugh, closed her eyes, and surrendered once again to the lips and tongue and body of her very own grand passion.

The End.

AUTHOR'S NOTE

I truly hope you enjoyed The Unwilling Smuggler. I enjoyed writing it!

If you did enjoy it, I would appreciate it if you left a review on Amazon or Goodreads.

If you're anything like me, you'll agree that writing reviews is a bit of a pain in the rear. I never know what to write, and wonder if I sound a bit vague or foolish. But believe me, reviews are ~almost~ as valuable as money for indie writers. And I will love you to pieces if you leave me one!

Reviews mean your favorite indie authors (including me) get to spend more time writing and less time worrying about sales and marketing! And that can only be good for *you*, because it means more book goodies can be created for you to enjoy!

I have taken one or two artistic liberties with history in the story, I hope you can forgive me!

First, while the smuggling gangs along the south coast of England were not averse to taking out retribution on informers, the gangs didn't necessarily have a policy of 'once you were in, you were always in'. Also, De Lacey's connections in London society would mean he would be offered more protection than the usual commoner. He would, more than likely, have been sent on his way with a hearty word of thanks and a pat on the back. And as long as he didn't tell any tales, he would have been left alone.

Second, the French emigres in London were more likely to socialize together than to try to enter London society. Someone of Eugenie's status would have been unlikely to be blithely accepted into society. Many English were suspicious of the French and even hostile that they were accepted and succored by the government, especially when they were given financial aid - which a good number of them were. Very few of the French brought sufficient funds to keep themselves for more than the couple of months they expected the revolution to last, even if they had budgeted, which they didn't.

There may be other anomalies, but for the sake of a cracking story, I'm happy to be lambasted for them... to a point. You can only be lambasted so much before it isn't fun any more.

There were, as always, a number of people who made this book totally amazing - first of all, my editor Melanie Cossey of Polished and Precise Editing Services. She takes my word vomits and turns them into lovely, lyrical sentences. I always say to myself "Wow, that's so much better! How come I didn't think of that?!?!?"

Romance Writers of Australia - an unbelievably talented and giving bunch of women (and seven or eight men) who prove every day that romance is alive and well and living the good life in Australia;

The online Indie community and especially the original members of 20BooksTo50K, who give so much information to everyone else so that they can succeed in this industry;

The best bunch of bitches - MJ, Katie, Wanika, Amber and Monique, and our other friend, Libby :-);

Finally, my incredible family - Aiden, who stoically accepts that his mum will be disappeared in fairy tales most the time, and my partner, Grant, without whom I would still be flailing madly through life. Love you both to pieces.

If you did enjoy The Unwilling Smuggler, you're going to *love* The Ruined Lady... the story of Felicity and Quincey. A little preview is on the following pages.

For now, thank you so much for reading.

Bree Verity.

Lady Felicity Merryweather knows her middling looks and moderate dowry mean she is unlikely ever to marry. So before she is consigned to a life of spinsterhood, she decides she will approach Quincey, Earl of Edenburgh, to show her the intimacies of life in one passionate, secret tryst. Her only condition - that he does not ask her to marry him following their interlude.

Quincey reluctantly agrees, never realizing that being with Felicity will awaken something new inside him.

When they are caught in a wholly innocent but compromising position, Quincey breaks his promise and asks for Felicity's hand. She refuses, thinking Quincey needs a society wife, not someone dowdy and plain as she.

When her parents discover she has refused the hand of an Earl, they organise a marriage for her to one of her father's business partners instead. And while Felicity accepts the engagement, she decides that she is going to completely be herself for her last few weeks in society.

What she doesn't expect is that an update of her wardrobe and a more talkative personality will make her an instant celebrity, and attract the attention of Lord Rushton, a known rake. She refuses his advances.

Quincey has reluctantly accepted his friend's advice to let Felicity go, and had found himself another potential bride, but no one shapes up to Felicity.

When Felicity's reputation is torn to shreds by Lord Rushton, Quincey jumps in to demand retribution.

Will Quincey be injured in the duel with Lord Rushton? And if he is not, will he ever be able to make Felicity understand that she is the perfect wife for him?

A friends-to-lover's romance that explores what it takes to ruin a reputation, and what it takes to redeem it again.

Turn the page for a preview of The Ruined Lady...

CHAPTER ONE

"I should like it very much… that is, if you would be so kind…"

Lady Felicity Merryweather was making a mess of the most important question of her life. It was taking too long, and Lord Edenburgh was starting to glaze over. She needed to come to the point, and quickly, before she lost her nerve. Mentally shaking the cobwebs from her head and the stutter from her voice, she fixed her pale blue eyes on the earl. Drawing a deep breath, she lifted her chin defiantly.

"I wish you to deflower me."

Lord Edenburgh choked on his brandy. He brought a fine linen handkerchief to his lips and for a few moments, was prisoner to a paroxysm of coughing. Felicity wondered if she should rush over and slap him on the back. Then his watering, shocked brown eyes lifted to meet with hers. "You wish me to what?"

"Deflower me. Take my virginity." She felt her blush rising, and worked to keep it subdued. It would not do for the earl to think she was embarrassed or ashamed.

"What, right now?" The earl was regarding her with all sorts of horror. Had the situation not been so critical, Felicity may well have laughed out loud at the dismay on his face.

"No, of course not. I mean, at an agreed upon time and place, we would meet and you would… deflower me."

Standing before the incredulous earl, Felicity started to wilt. Perhaps this had not been such a good idea after all. Her unbecoming flush rose again. Even the word - deflower - seemed to be foolish. Clipping roses from a bush was one thing. This was very much another.

And yet Felicity stood her ground, resolute in her decision. She knew she would never marry - her modest dowry, ridiculous red hair, freckles and gangly limbs made sure of that - and so as the season began, Felicity decided to gift herself one night of passion before settling down into dreary spinsterhood.

Once the decision had been taken, all that was left was to determine the perfect partner in her tryst. She had confided her wish to her dear friend, Lady Juliet Hampshire who, after a first moment of doubtful surprise, quickly warmed to the idea and provided some shrewd advice. Lady Hampshire, after all, was a widow, with a reputed long line of lovers behind her. They had been friends for several years, and Felicity trusted her judgment and understanding of the delicacy of the situation.

"He must be someone you can trust implicitly," she had told Felicity seriously. "Understand that you place your reputation into the hands of the gentleman. You must be sure he will treat it with due care." Felicity had nodded, eager for her friend's wisdom.

"He must be someone you are physically attracted to. If he is to be the only man you ever lie with, you do not want your memories to be tarnished with visions of his protruding stomach or bad teeth." Felicity had shuddered.

"And he must be someone you are sure will treat you gently during the affair. A libertine, or a profligate will use your body for his own pleasure only. Choose a man who you believe will be willing to allow you your pleasure as well." Now, Felicity had been blushing. Juliet had taken her by the arm, chuckling. "Oh, my dear, are you sure this is what you want? You are such an innocent."

Now, standing in front of the earl as his eyes traveled from her too-big feet to her plainly-decorated straw hat, she had to agree. She was innocent - in fact, far too innocent for any six-and-twenty year old woman. She needed to have this experience, before she dwindled into a life of spinsterhood and regrets.

She peeked up at the earl, who was even now shakily reaching for another glass of brandy. Timidly, she asked, "Do you think you could accommodate me, my lord?"

His rough laugh startled her. "Good god, Felicity, if you're going to come in here and stand in front of my desk and ask me to bed you, at least call me Quincey."

She smiled. "Quincey, then. What do you think?"

He turned to face her. "I think you are the most addle-pated female I have ever met." Scowling, he downed the brandy in one gulp.

Felicity tried not to smile. His instant refusal had been expected. Now it was time to make her case.

"Quincey, I understand you might be a little surprised by my request. Stunned, even," she quickly added, as he threw her an incredulous look. "However I have considered this course long and hard, and I do believe it is the correct one for me."

The earl sat heavily into his chair behind his desk, rolling his eyes, and groaning, "Long and hard. God help me." Felicity frowned at his words, but pressed on.

"It is quite apparent to me that I shall never marry. Unfortunately, I am a little too... plain and awkward to attract the kinds of gentleman I think I might like." She grimaced, sweeping a hand down her front. "A skinny, ugly, old maid. That is what I am become." At the earl's weak protest, Felicity shook her head. "Oh, no, Quincey, it is quite alright. I am accepting of my fate. Except for one single facet."

"And so we swing back around to it," replied the earl heavily.

"Yes. All I ask for is one night to experience what every other woman takes for granted. And then, we shall forget it ever happened, you will go on to find yourself a lovely, society wife, and I will molder into spinsterhood."

Even when she spoke so frankly about it, Felicity hated the words. It hurt to know she had been rejected by so many men based entirely on her looks. Very few gentleman had even tried to scratch the surface, none had dug deep enough to meet the real Felicity.

Quincey, of course, didn't count amongst the throngs of disinterested men. As a family friend, she had grown up with him, watched as he became Viscount Healey, and then commiserated with him on the attainment of the Earldom, as it meant the demise of the rest of his family. He had never expected to become the earl. His uncle had a stalwart son, and seemed to be the very epitome of health. Sadly, his heart had failed him when he had discovered that his son, the honorable

Reginald, had been killed in a drunken duel over some other man's wife. Quincey was left to take up the reins of the Earldom, which he had done with the understated efficiency and enthusiasm that had always been his way.

Quincey never commented on her looks, either to say she looked nice, or that she didn't. Felicity thought he simply didn't see. She was a background ornament, an ugly vase that sat on a pedestal in the back rooms of his life. Like a hideous family heirloom that was always there, and always overlooked.

She thought that now, Quincey was actually looking at her, and the sensation was a little disconcerting.

"What are you thinking, Quincey?"

She took a seat on a low sofa, placing her shaking hands in her lap and crossing her ankles demurely. She could no longer look Quincey in the eye, nor deny the riot of pink that flushed through her cheeks. She must look a sight. She was not one of those lovely females whose blushes looked like the kisses of angels. No, her flush was more like a slap in the face from the devil himself. It burned bright pink, in dreadful combination with her bright red hair. She sighed. Quincey's silence spoke volumes. He was going to reject her.

In her peripheral vision, she saw Quincey heave himself out of his chair and come to sit beside her. Taking her hands, he asked kindly, "Is this really what you want?"

Her eyes flew up to meet his, warm and light brown in his boyish face. Familiar eyes, that she had looked at many times before. Why had she never noticed the tiny darts of copper running through them?

"Yes." The one word was solid, with no traces of nerves in her voice.

"And you are certain it will not be something you will regret afterward?"

She gave a short laugh. "That I cannot answer. However, I do know that I will regret it my entire life if I do not do it."

He nodded, then stilled, and his grip on her hands grew a little tighter. "Why me, Felicity?"

She moistened her dry lips, and gave him a wavering smile. "Because you are my friend," she replied simply.

The earl breathed in deeply, then blew the breath out in a huff. Felicity smelled brandy and pipe smoke on his breath, comforting, familiar scents. He scratched his head, his brows drawn and his mouth a hard line.

To Felicity's surprise, he jumped up and walked rapidly around the room. Then, he spun toward her accusingly. "This is an enormous responsibility you wish to place on me you know, Felicity?"

She nodded silently.

"You come in here, asking me this, when I've only ever thought of you as a neighbour and a friend - not ever as an actual woman."

She nodded again. That was something of which she was acutely aware. "I know."

"And now you want me to…" he waved his hand in her direction, "and then we would… it's preposterous! Preposterous!" He glared at her, and she calmly looked back at him, waiting.

Quincey's chest heaved in irritation, but Felicity merely allowed the question to hang in the air. If there was one thing she knew about Quincey, it was that he blustered and bellowed just before he came to a difficult decision.

He strode back around to his desk chair. "Have you no thought for your reputation? For your parents? For me?"

"Of course. Nobody's reputation needs to suffer. Only you and I ever need ever know it even happened."

He gaped at her, then seemed to deflate, falling into his chair.

"I cannot believe I'm considering this," he groaned, putting his head into his hands. Felicity waited.

Then he looked up challengingly, directly into Felicity's eyes.

"Very well. I'll do it."

The Ruined Lady is available on Amazon for pre-order - follow this QR code for more information:

www.ingramcontent.com/pod-product-compliance
Lightning Source LLC
Chambersburg PA
CBHW031309120626
46554CB00001BA/351

* 9 7 8 0 6 4 8 1 5 1 7 0 8 *